The *Accidental* Mail Order Bride

Chance at Love Series: Book 3

The *Accidental* Mail Order Bride

Ruth Ann Nordin

Wedded Bliss Romances, LLC

Wedded Bliss Romances, LLC
http://www.ruthannnordin.com

Dedication: To Sharon Fournier who has a kind heart and a wonderful sense of humor. Thanks for giving me a reason to smile!

Chapter One

First week of August 1878
Colorado

Allison Jones stepped off the stagecoach, relieved the long journey had finally come to an end. With all the swaying of the stagecoach for the past week, she felt as if she was still rocking from side to side, so it took a moment to gather her balance.

Assured everything around her wasn't jiggling around, she focused on the group who were gathered around her, most at a good distance. Three of the people approached her. A white man and woman with a black child. She glanced around, wondering if the man she was supposed to marry was anywhere in the group, but the woman spoke, directing her attention back to the three people.

"Are you Miss Allison Jones?" the woman asked, her southern drawl similar to hers.

"Yes, but you may call me Allie," she replied. Glancing between the woman and man, she added, "Do you know where I can find Sheriff Eric Johnson?"

"I'm him," the man said.

"Oh?" Allie took another good look at the woman standing next to him. It didn't seem as if they were related. They looked too different. In fact, when she caught the way they looked at each other, it was apparent the two were in love. "Are you the Eric Johnson who's expecting me?"

"Yes, I am," Eric replied. "But the day you were supposed to arrive, Caroline came instead, and she brought this young boy with her." He gestured to the child, who seemed to be studying her with interest. "I thought you were her, and I married her before I realized she wasn't you."

Allie forced her gaze off of the child and returned it to the couple.

"I didn't realize he was the wrong gentleman," Caroline added, an apologetic tone in her voice. "I was supposed to go to Georgetown and marry someone else. Caleb," she motioned to the child, "wasn't feeling well, and I was distracted with trying to care for him." She paused. "I'm sorry, Allie. I never intended to take your place."

The realization of what they were saying was finally sinking in, and Allie wasn't sure what to do. She brushed a wisp of her golden hair from her eyes and scanned the crowd. They still kept their distance, but she wasn't sure if they could hear everything that was going on or not.

"I know this is awkward," Eric said. "It all happened so fast, and I just got the last missive you sent a few days ago."

He pulled out a folded paper from his pocket and showed it to her. She opened it, and sure enough, it was the missive she'd written to him explaining why she'd been delayed in Missouri. She slowly folded it. What was she supposed to do now? She couldn't go back to Tennessee. Her future hinged on being here.

"There is a bachelor," Eric continued. "He lives out that way." He pointed to the north. "He's a good man. He's twenty-three and has thirty acres of land. He takes care of odds and ends."

She waited for him to explain what he meant by "odds and ends".

Instead, he said, "Travis is quiet and shy, so it'll take him time to get used to you. But I assure you, he's gentle and kind, and he'll treat you well."

She glanced at Caroline, who gave her an encouraging nod.

"He's lonely," the boy spoke up. "He needs someone to love."

Eric patted the boy's shoulder. "Caleb's right. Travis would benefit from marriage."

Once again, turning her gaze to the crowd, Allie asked, "Where is he?"

"He's not here," Eric replied. "To be honest, we didn't tell him you were coming."

She frowned. This didn't sound promising. "Why not?"

"Travis," Caroline began, "has a tendency to run from ladies. He ran from me when I came to his property to help Eric. I had to go to the building and knock on the door to get him to listen to me. Once he realized Eric needed his help, he came right out to assist him."

"Right," Eric added. "He's the kind of person who'll go out of his way to help others when he can. I know you're like that, too, because you stayed in Missouri to testify in a murder trial. He would have done the same thing. We think you'll be a good match."

"Oh, well…" Allie ran her fingers along the edge of the missive. Should she do it? Should she go out to Travis' home and marry him? She hadn't even written to him. He was more of a stranger to her than Eric had been. She cleared her throat. "Is there anyone else I might marry?"

Like someone who was right here where she could see him and talk to him before making a decision?

She scanned the group, who still kept their distance. There were some men of marriageable age there. Did they already have wives?

"I'm afraid there's no one else," Eric told her, bringing her attention back to him. "They either have wives or are too old to be a suitable match for you. And, unfortunately, this town is so small the only employment you could get is at the saloon."

She frowned as she caught his meaning. She'd heard stories of men going to saloons to seek an evening's pleasure with a soiled dove, but she had no desire to do that kind of thing. She didn't know how many women would be happy doing it. Probably none.

"Well," she began, trying not to give into defeat. It'd been a long and tiring trip, and now things were worse since she'd been delayed in coming here. She'd thought the worst of it was behind her. But now she'd just learned another thing had gone wrong. "I suppose I don't have a choice but to marry the only bachelor in town."

"Travis is a good man," Eric said. "I assure you, it'll work out."

Despite his reassuring smile, she wasn't convinced. Not fully. What kind of man made it a point of hiding from women?

Caroline seemed to pick up on her uncertainty, for she rested a hand on her arm. "I don't blame you for being scared," she whispered. "The prospect of marrying someone you never met is absolutely frightening. I just hope it helps to know you're marrying a good and honorable gentleman. He'll be kind to you."

Allie wanted to tell her she appreciated Caroline's concern, but the words wouldn't come out. All she could hope for was that Eric, Caroline, and the boy were right.

"Alright then," Eric said. "I'll get your things and put them in the wagon. Then we'll get the judge and head on out."

Judge? Allie turned to him as he went to the stagecoach. "But I thought there'd be a preacher to conduct the ceremony."

"There was one here when you were supposed to come in," Eric replied, offering an apologetic smile. "But he hasn't been back since. I'm afraid the judge is the best I can do."

Oh. Though Allie didn't consider herself to be the superstitious kind, it seemed like a bad omen to be married by a judge instead of a preacher.

"The wagon is over there," Caroline told her.

Reluctant, Allie followed Caroline's gaze and saw the nearby wagon with two horses ready to take her to her new home. God only knew what waited for her, and truth be told, she didn't want to find out.

***

With a grunt, Travis Martin pounded the stake into the ground until it was secure. Out of breath, he wiped the sweat from his forehead. He'd been working all morning to get this fence set up, and at long last, he had one more post to go. Just as he bent down to get the last post, he heard horses pulling a wagon up to his property.

Stiffening, he saw the wagon through the trees along the winding path that lead up to his property. He squinted as he tried to figure out who was coming. After a moment, he realized it was Eric, his wife, their boy, and... His eyes grew wide. Another woman was there. And there was no man with her.

He threw the post to the ground and hurried up the side of the hill. This wasn't good. He hadn't brought a hat with him, and he wasn't even wearing a shirt. In fact, he wasn't even wearing his undershirt! So few people ever came out here. Why did this day have to be the one when someone did?

He dodged around the trees, managing to stay hidden from their view. Fortunately, he reached the building before they pulled up to the cottage. Out of breath, he threw on his undershirt. Too late, he remembered that he hadn't brought out his shirt and hat to the building.

With a groan, he wiped his dark hair away from his eyes and glanced out the small window which had a perfect view of his cottage. Eric pulled on the reins of the horses, and the wagon came to a stop. Usually, he didn't mind it when Eric came out here, but Eric knew how he felt about bringing women out to his property.

It was one thing to show his scarred face and monstrous frame to a man. It was something else to offend a woman's delicate sensibilities by exposing her to someone as ugly as himself.

To his horror, another person came up onto his property. It was a man on a horse. And if he saw right, the middle-aged man was the judge. Why would Eric be bringing a judge with him? Travis hadn't done anything wrong.

Then Travis remembered Abe's visit the previous month. Abe had told him about Eric marrying the wrong woman. Apparently, his mail-order bride hadn't shown up when she was supposed to. Travis knew so little of what happened in town, but he knew there were very few women, especially ones in their early twenties.

Now, he couldn't be sure, but he had a nagging suspicion the blonde-haired beautiful woman stepping down from the wagon was supposed to have been Eric's bride. And that was bad. Really bad. Eric had never brought a woman out here before, except for the one time he needed help with Lydia's dead body.

Travis watched as the judge got off his horse. Scooting away from the window, Travis went to the door and opened it a crack so he could hear what they were saying.

"Are you sure this is a good idea?" the blonde woman asked.

It had to be the blonde asking since he didn't recognize her voice out of everyone lurking outside his cottage.

"I'm sure." That was Eric. "Travis will be a good husband to you."

Travis' jaw dropped. Eric couldn't be serious. Didn't he know what people thought about him? Didn't he pay attention to all the rumors that circulated through town? Travis rarely ever made it to town, and he knew what those folks were saying. Surely, Eric had some notion of it, too.

Someone knocked on the door of his cottage, and everyone waited in silence for a good minute before the judge said, "I don't think he's here."

"Of course," Eric replied with a laugh. "He stays busy. He wouldn't be in his home while there's work to be done. I bet he's in his barn or his workshop."

Travis grimaced. Why did Eric have to know him so well? And this brought up the same question Travis had before. Why would Eric willingly bring a lovely young woman out here to marry him when he knew full well how hideous he was? Didn't he care at all about her? She ought to be spared the misery. Especially an entire lifetime of it.

Footsteps made him bolt straight up. He had to hide! But where? At the moment, he was trapped in this building. He'd never fit through the small windows.

He turned back to the piles of wood, scraps, and other odds and ends that he used to make things. Was there a suitable hiding place somewhere in all this rubble?

A knock came at the door behind him. Without thinking, he darted behind a pile of wood and knelt behind it. It didn't cover him completely, but it'd have to do.

"Travis?" Eric called out from the other side of the door.

Travis didn't answer. Maybe if he kept quiet, they'd all go away.

That, unfortunately, didn't happen because he heard the door creak open. Travis grimaced. Why hadn't he ever put a lock on that door?

"It's just me, Travis," Eric told him, shutting the door behind him.

Travis continued to keep quiet. With any luck, Eric would assume he wasn't there and leave.

"I can see the top of your head from behind that wood pile," Eric said.

Just his luck. Eric was much too observant. "I'm not fully dressed," Travis replied, not bothering to come out. "My hat and shirt are in the cottage."

"Is that all? Well, I can get those for you."

"What do you want?" Travis asked.

Eric might as well come out with it. If he intended to ruin a poor woman's life, he ought to admit it. But even as Travis thought this, he was hoping Eric would have a change of heart. He was hoping Eric would make up some excuse, like needing a piece of wood or metal, before taking the woman to some other man who could marry her.

Eric let out a tentative chuckle. "The funniest thing happened. You see, the mail-order bride I was expecting finally came in. She was delayed in Missouri. She saw someone kill another person on the train and had to stay in town to testify in court."

Leave it to Eric to not get to the point. Abe would just come out and say what he wanted, but Eric liked to talk. Usually, that wouldn't bother him. But today, Eric hadn't come to ask for his help with a dead body or making arrangements for a funeral.

"Actually," Eric continued, "I came because I think you and Allie will be good together."

"Allie?"

"Allison Jones. She likes to be called Allie. She's from Tennessee. There's a lot of poverty in that part of the country. Anyway, she has no way to support herself. I was going to marry her, but then Caroline came. Well, you know how that worked out. I married Caroline, and since that's the case, I can't marry Allie."

"I'm not marrying her," Travis blurted out, figuring he might as well just come out and say it. Why prolong the inevitable?

"Now, you didn't let me finish."

"I don't need to. I'm not marrying her. I'm not marrying anyone. I like being alone."

"Hold on. Let me finish."

"What's the point? The answer isn't going to change."

As if Travis hadn't spoken, Eric said, "Allie's real good at cooking. I know you like the food Lois makes. You're always bartering things to get something from her. Wouldn't it be even better if you could have a nice, home cooked meal every day? Why, you wouldn't have just one meal. You'd have two. Or maybe even three. She enjoys being in the kitchen."

"I eat just fine already," Travis replied. Really, if Eric thought he was so simple he'd agree to the marriage for that reason, he was sorely mistaken.

"Allie's also good at housekeeping. I notice you do a lot of things outside. You keep busy with all the projects you have going on in this workshop. That doesn't leave you with much time to tidy the cottage up. Wouldn't it be nice to have someone here to do that for you?"

"No."

"What about your laundry? Can you honestly tell me you like washing your clothes and bedding all the time?"

"I only do it once a month."

After a long pause, Eric let out a frustrated groan. "Come on, Travis. Marriage will be a good thing for you. Take it from a recently married man. There's nothing better than having a wife. Even if you don't care about having someone cook and clean for you, you would benefit from the companionship. It has to get lonely out here."

"I do just fine."

"Not according to Caleb."

"Caleb?" What did the seven-year-old child have to do with this?

"Caleb says you're lonely, and Caleb's never wrong when it comes to figuring people out."

"Caleb doesn't know what he's talking about," Travis snapped. Then, taking a moment to calm down, he added, "I meant no disrespect. It's just that the boy is wrong. I'm not lonely. I came out here because I wanted to be alone. I like it that way."

A long pause passed between them, and Travis thought that maybe—hopefully—Eric was finally going to stop this nonsense about him getting married.

"He is only seven," Eric conceded. "And you know better than anyone whether or not you're lonely." After a moment, he added, "Alright. I suppose I'll go out there and tell Allie you won't marry her."

"Good. She'll be better off."

Eric removed his hat, wiped his brow, and then put it back on. "I hope so."

Travis frowned as Eric turned to head for the door. He knew he shouldn't ask the question, but something in Eric's tone told him he was worried. "What do you mean you hope so?"

Even as he asked the question, he kicked himself for it. This was a trap. That's all it was. Eric was playing him. But it was like finding that dead body in the ravine. Travis hadn't wanted to look, but he'd felt compelled to.

Eric didn't turn back to him. He stared at the door, his shoulders slumped. "I don't want to trouble you with it. It's not your problem. It's mine. I just need to figure out a way to tell her she needs to work at the saloon."

"What?" Travis bolted up without even thinking. Realizing his error, he quickly crouched back down. "She won't have to work at the saloon."

Eric shook his head as he turned back toward Travis. "I'm afraid there's no other choice. Carl Richie has already posted a mail-order bride ad, and I heard he got a response yesterday when the mail came in. You're the only bachelor of marrying age left in this town. Allie can't go back home. She's got a full family. After the war, they lost nearly everything and have been struggling. She came out here to make a better life for herself. You ever gone to bed hungry, Travis?"

Travis knew he was going to regret answering, but he did anyway. "No."

"Well, I have, and I can tell you it's a hard thing to go through. It's even worse when you don't know where your next meal is going to come from. She can't go back. Her family is barely hanging on as it is. The last thing they need is another mouth to feed. Anyway, like I said, it isn't your problem. It's mine."

"Why can't you hire her to help you and Caroline out?"

"You don't know much about women, do you?"

"I don't know anything about women." He was surprised Eric even asked such a ridiculous thing. "My mother died when I was two."

"Oh, in that case, you really don't. The thing is, I was supposed to marry Allie, but I married Caroline instead. Things would be too awkward if I hired Allie to help Caroline. I'm sure they'd make an effort to get along, but it'd be awkward nonetheless." Eric shrugged. "I'll see if the saloon owner will be easy on her. You know, not give her too many customers in a night. She hasn't known a man before. She'll need to be gently led into the business."

Travis let out a heavy sigh. Great. Eric was laying the guilt trip on pretty thick, and worse, Travis was falling for it. "You're an impossible man to deal with, Sheriff."

"It's only right I insist the owner go easy on her." Then, probably sensing he'd done his part to make Travis feel bad for her, Eric headed for the door.

"That's not what I meant, and you know it."

If Travis was smart, he'd call Eric's bluff. He wouldn't have to marry Allie, and Allie would be spared a lifetime of misery with him. But there was that small—albeit very small—chance Eric might be telling the truth. And God help him, but Travis couldn't have that on his conscience.

When Eric reached for the doorknob, Travis groaned. "Alright, I'll marry her. But one thing we better get straight, and we got to do it right away. I won't have anything to do with her. She can stay in the cottage. I'm staying out here. So you need to get all my clothes out of there and bring them here."

"Why don't you just pull your hat low over your face so she can't see you?"

"This is the deal I'm making. You want me to save her from the saloon and starvation? Then we're going to do this my way."

"You're right. I'll do what you say."

Good. At least Travis was having one thing go his way. "Like I said, I want all of my clothes out here. I'll also need one of my blankets. You'll have to provide me with some paper and a pencil." After a moment, he asked, "She knows how to read and write, doesn't she?"

"She does."

Eric turned to leave, and this time Travis let him. God help him. God help Allie. He was about to make a vow to trap them both into a situation neither one would be happy in.

Chapter Two

"He's a nice person," Caroline was saying—again—while Allie and the judge waited.

Caleb, who was chasing a rabbit, was spared Caroline's relentless speech on how good Travis was.

Allie's stomach kept twisting into knots. The fact that Eric and Caroline wanted her to marry a man who hid in the building as soon as he saw them wasn't promising. It wasn't promising at all. All Allie could remember was how large he was. He had to be about six and a half feet tall, and he was built like a bear.

"I'm wasting my time out here," the judge muttered. "The sheriff is taking longer than a woman getting ready for church."

"That's only because Travis is terribly shy," Caroline replied. "Eric's taking the time to explain the situation to him."

"Travis ought to be glad anyone's willing to marry him," the judge said. "No other woman would be brave enough."

"Is that true?" Allie asked, turning her gaze to Caroline. Was Travis so horrible no one would have him?

Caroline let out a long sigh. "You might as well know the truth, Allie. People around here have made up all kinds of rumors about Travis, but those rumors aren't true."

"What are they saying about him?" Allie asked.

"Nothing that matters," Caroline quickly replied. "They speak nothing but nonsense."

"You might as well let her know what she's getting herself into by marrying him," the judge told Caroline. "She's going to hear the rumors sooner or later."

Caroline hesitated, shifting from one foot to another, before saying, "No good comes from rumors. They're laced with lies."

"Even so, Allie has a right to know since they're about the man she's going to marry." The judge faced Allie. "No one's seen Travis' parents. It's as if he appeared here one day and took up residence. The couple who lived here before reportedly sold this place to him and headed on out, but no one saw them leave."

"Well, I hadn't heard anything about the people who lived here before Travis did," Caroline said.

"I knew the couple. A kindly elderly husband and wife who built this homestead before the gold and silver rush. They had three children who all moved away."

"How sad," Caroline replied.

"It is, especially since a year after the youngest left, they seemed to disappear. No one heard from them after that. One day they were here. Another, Travis had taken up residence."

"What are you implying?" Allie asked, sensing there was something he wasn't telling her.

"I don't want to upset anyone's sensibilities, but it is strange they were never seen or heard from again," the judge said. "Not a single missive. No good-byes. Nothing."

"Maybe the people left and figured it was no one's business," Caroline objected.

The judge turned to Caroline. "I realize you need to think that because you're planning to marry this young woman to him, but it doesn't change facts."

"Are you saying you think he killed those people so he could live here?" Allie asked.

"No one can say anything for sure," the judge replied. "It's just strange, that's all. That couple knew people in town. If they left, why didn't they tell anyone?"

Caroline put her hand on her hip and shot the judge a pointed look. "Because this town is full of busybodies who have nothing better to do with their time than to gossip. I'm surprised at you. I would think you'd know better since you're a judge."

"I'm not making up rumors," the judge said, his tone indignant. "I'm stating facts. And the facts are that the couple was here one day and gone the next. No one knows how or why. Now," his gaze went to Allie, "as for the things people are saying about the man you're about to marry, I think you have every right to know what those rumors are. Don't you?"

Allie's heartbeat picked up in dread. Yes, she did. But did she really want to know?

Without giving Allie time to decide, he said, "Some people say he has only one human parent. The other parent is a spirit or some kind of monster lurking these parts."

"Please lower your voice," Caroline told the judge. "I don't want Caleb hearing any of this."

"You're right," the judge conceded. "We don't want to frighten the child."

Allie's eyes widened. Frighten the child? Caroline and Eric wanted her to marry a man who could frighten children?

"Some people say," the judge continued, "he is hideous to look at. He has a beastly face. That's why he hides it as much as possible. And it's a good thing, too, they say, because if you look directly at his face, something bad will happen to you."

Caroline groaned. "Nonsense. This is all nonsense. I looked at him myself, and nothing bad happened to me."

"Are you saying he doesn't have ghastly markings on his face?"

"Scars." Caroline's gaze went to Allie, her expression pleading with Allie to believe her. "They're only scars."

"Scars from what?" the judge pressed.

Caroline shrugged. "I don't know."

"Then how can you say there's nothing strange about them? Maybe when you looked at him, you were bewitched. Maybe he only made you think you saw scars. Maybe he really is a beast in appearance. He could have three eyes or two noses. Maybe he's missing a mouth."

Allie gasped. Could such a person possibly exist?

Caroline shook her head in irritation. "I would think someone who is a judge would have better sense than to say such things." She turned to Allie. "Don't pay him any mind. He doesn't know what he's saying."

"It's what the people in this town are saying, not me," he replied.

"You're just as bad as they are by repeating it," Caroline hissed, her polite demeanor quickly giving way to anger.

"She has a right to know," the judge said, choosing to speak slowly as if Caroline didn't understand him the other times he'd told her this.

"She has a right to know the truth, and you're not telling her the truth," Caroline insisted.

The door of the building opened, and Eric came out. Allie held her breath, waiting to see if the monster…the man they wanted her to marry…would come out, too. If she could see him for herself, she'd feel much better about this whole thing. As it was, her stomach was tensing up into all sorts of horrible knots.

This wasn't good. It wasn't good at all. Her luck had gone from bad to worse. If only she hadn't been delayed in Missouri. Then she would have married Eric, and this wouldn't even be an issue now. Caroline could have married him instead. Judging by Caroline's persistence in defending him, she would have been a much better choice.

Eric shut the door behind him, signaling Allie would not get to see Travis after all. She didn't know if that was good or not. While she had to see what he looked like so she could know the truth, she was afraid to find out.

"Good news," Eric said, looking directly at her, seeming very pleased with what he was about to tell her. "Travis has agreed to marry you."

Caroline let out an audible sigh of relief. "That is good."

Allie glanced at the judge to see if he would argue that this wasn't good news, but he kept quiet. Why was it he'd felt free to voice his opinion only moments ago? Was the fact that Eric was standing in front of him preventing him from doing so? Allie didn't know how much influence a sheriff had this far out west, but she did know they had significant influence where she'd grown up.

"Travis did have some requests," Eric continued.

Noting the hesitation in his voice, Allie's attention went back to him. "Oh?" As much as she hated to find out what those requests were, she felt compelled to ask. "What does he want?"

"He's a little insecure about his looks," Eric began.

The judge's eyebrows raised in a way that indicated "a little insecure" was an understatement, but he kept his mouth shut.

"He has some scars on his face," Eric said, his voice lower, probably so Travis wouldn't overhear. "It's nothing bad, though some in town will make it out to be as if it is."

"Exactly," Caroline chimed in. "I've seen him for myself, and people exaggerate."

"But you won't even have to worry about seeing him," Eric told Allie. "He will give you the cottage all to yourself, and he'll live in the building." He gestured to the building he'd just come from.

Allie's stomach tensed. That didn't sound like something a normal man would want. A normal man would want to share the cottage with his wife.

"He's shy around women," Eric explained as if he could read her mind. "I'm sure once he gets used to having you around, he'll want to go back to the cottage. In the meantime, I told him I'd take his clothes out to the building. Ron, you mind helping me?"

"When will we be getting on with the wedding?" the judge—Ron—asked.

"As soon as we get his things out there." He nodded to the building.

Ron shrugged. "Why not? It's better than waiting out here."

Looking far too happy about this, Eric hurried over to the wagon and took Allie's trunk from it. "You should come in and look around since this is going to be your home," Eric called out to her as he made a beeline straight for the small home hidden by trees.

Despite her apprehension, Allie forced her feet forward, Caroline joining her. Caroline was saying something about how quaint a cottage was, but Allie wasn't paying attention. She was finally taking note of her surroundings, and the entire place seemed to be in a state of despair. Weeds covered most of the landscape, preventing flowers from flourishing here. Vines crawled up the sides of the barn, building, and even the cottage as if they wished to consume them.

Once she slipped past the trees, she realized the branches blocked out most of the sunlight, making her feel as if it'd just become twilight. She shivered and wrapped her arms around herself. This cottage wasn't the least bit quaint. She didn't even know how Caroline could think such a thing. There was nothing charming or pretty about it.

It's because she doesn't have to marry Travis. It's easier to see the good in things when you're not the one who has to go through it.

"Ron, get the door," Eric told the judge.

The judge did as he asked, and the wooden door creaked on its hinges.

Allie slowed to a stop and took a deep breath to steel her resolve. She had nowhere else to go. Her family could no longer afford to take care of her.

There weren't enough men to find a husband back in Tennessee. The West, however, was teeming with them. With all the single men who'd come out to find fortunes in gold and silver, there was a lack of women. It seemed like a safe bet. The men needed women to tend to their homes, and women needed men to provide for them.

"Surely, the man you marry will be so grateful to have you that he'll be good to you," her mother had told her as they packed her things.

But the man she was about to marry didn't seem at all interested in her, and she doubted he was grateful to have someone there to help him.

"Come on," Caroline gently urged.

Allie glanced back at the wagon. What other choice did she have? No other man had responded to any of her replies. Eric had been the only one, and she'd had the impression he was a good, decent man. That impression had been right. She could tell that he made a good husband by the way he treated Caroline. He loved her. He cherished her. And he'd ended up with her all because Allie had made the decision to stay in Missouri and testify before a jury.

Allie wanted to resent Caroline for getting to Eric before she could. Really, she did. But Caroline had such a sweet disposition that Allie couldn't hate her. And for some reason, that only made her feel worse about her own predicament.

The men went into the cottage, but Allie lingered outside. Once she stepped inside, this whole thing would be real. She wouldn't be able to turn back.

She turned to Caroline, who stood next to her. "There's no other option for me? There's really not another bachelor or…or…a job I can get?"

Caroline put her arm around her shoulders. "I'm afraid all the marriageable bachelors are taken. Well, there is one who recently became available, but his wife was murdered so I'm not sure that's an ideal choice."

Murder? Someone was going around murdering people in this town? Was it…could it be… Travis didn't go around killing people, did he? Allie would have asked this if her throat hadn't gone dry. Maybe that was why people were afraid of him. Maybe they had a reason to be afraid. Caroline and Eric could be wrong about him. What if Travis seemed nice to them but really wasn't? How could an entire town—and a judge—be wrong about him?

"As for jobs," Caroline added, not seeming to notice Allie's growing unease, "this town doesn't present any worthwhile opportunities to ladies. The only job you could get is at the saloon, and Eric told me this wouldn't be a good thing."

No. It wouldn't. Allie had heard about prostitutes who worked in saloons.

"I can see the judge has frightened you," Caroline said. "I wish he hadn't done that. Allie, I promise you, Travis is a good man. You have nothing to worry about."

"Are you coming in?" Eric called out.

"Yes, we're coming," Caroline replied, sounding just as chipper as Eric.

Well, maybe the two were well-matched after all. They shared the same ridiculous optimism.

Allie followed Caroline into the cottage. The place was even darker than it'd been outside because the curtains were drawn, preventing any light from making its way in.

The judge struck a match and lit the kerosene lamp in the kitchen, and Allie had almost wished he hadn't because now she could see the dust that covered the curtains and the unused dishes and shelves in the kitchen.

"It's a bachelor's home," Caroline told Allie. "You need to keep that in mind."

The judge rolled his eyes, and Allie had to agree with him. The place seemed much more suitable for a beast than a human.

"Let's see the rest of it," Caroline said, still not missing a beat in her cheerful demeanor.

The judge led the way out of the kitchen, and since Caroline smiled expectantly at her, Allie proceeded forward.

The parlor was similar to the kitchen. The furniture had seen better days, and most of the room had gone unused, which meant more dirt and dust. There were even dirty footprints on the floor from where Travis had brought mud into the house. With a glance back, she noted the floor in the kitchen had the same telltale signs he hadn't taken his boots off before entering the house. Oh heavens. She had her work cut out for her. Even with a large family, she couldn't recall seeing so much to clean up.

Eric lugged a basket with a pile of clothes, a blanket, a hat, and grooming supplies. Her eyes widened. Grooming supplies? Travis took the time to comb his hair and shave? She was shocked since he didn't bother taking care of anything else around here.

"Your trunk is in the bedroom," Eric told her. "You can put your things anywhere you want."

Since everyone expected her to check the room out, she did, dragging her feet the entire way. The bed was larger than she'd expected it to be, but maybe he needed a big bed because he was large. She recalled how tall and broad he was. Yes, a small bed wouldn't have fit him.

The sheets and blankets on the bed weren't made, something that didn't surprise her after seeing the rest of the house. The floor was cleaner in here, though, indicating he at least had the sense to remove his boots before coming into this room. She inspected the rest of the room. There was something missing, but she couldn't put her finger on it. It seemed to have everything a person would expect. A bed, a dresser, and a washbasin. There was even a small wardrobe to hang things in and a shelf to set hats on. So what was it?

"You want to see the last room?" Caroline asked.

She might as well get this over with. Allie left the bedroom and went to the last room, which also happened to be a bedroom, except this had two beds, a small dresser, and hooks on the wall to hang things. All of these went unused. But there was something she noticed in this room that had been missing in the other one. There was a sheet draped over a large circular object above the dresser.

Curious, she went over to it and lifted it, sneezing as the dust rose up and met her nose. She wiped her eyes then took a look at what was behind the sheet. A mirror. That's what was missing from the other bedroom! A mirror.

She returned to the other bedroom. Her gaze went to the dresser, and she saw that the dresser had, at one time, held a mirror. There were missing screws, telling her it'd been removed. She inwardly shivered. If all Travis had were some scars, why did he take away this mirror and cover up the other one? What kind of man couldn't even bear to look at himself?

She glanced at Caroline who was tidying up the bed. She had the nagging suspicion that Eric and Caroline were lying to her. Travis had to have more than scars on his face. Even if the rumors were exaggerated, certainly there was some truth in them.

Eric returned, still smiling as if this was a joyous event. "Alright. I think we're ready for the wedding."

"I can come here and help you clean this place up," Caroline told Allie. "Once we get rid of the dust and cobwebs, it'll be lovely."

Cobwebs? Allie's gaze went up, and sure enough, she spotted several of them along the ceiling. Looking down, she noted they were also along the corners of the floor. Everything about this place was dirty. She didn't know whether to scream or cry.

Oh why—oh why!—couldn't she have ended up with someone other than Travis?

Caroline put her arm around her shoulders and led her out of the bedroom. Caroline probably figured Allie needed a good nudge in order to go through with this. And Caroline was right. If there was some way she could get out of this marriage, she'd hop in the wagon and lead the horses back to town herself. But there was nowhere else she could go. She was stuck here.

When they were out of the cottage, Allie stopped. She had a sinking feeling this was going to be a disaster. But what choice did she have? At least this way, she had a roof over her head and would be left alone.

She supposed the only saving grace was that Travis was willing to leave her alone. He wouldn't be living in this cottage with her. Releasing a shaky breath, she said a quick prayer then marched forward to her doom.

Chapter Three

Travis had just put on a shirt and his hat that Eric had brought out to him when he saw the group coming toward the building. Just as he feared. They were really going to go through with this. He blocked the door with a large piece of scrap metal and waited for them. There was no way he was going out there. The judge would have to perform the ceremony—such as it was—with a door between them. This was now his only safe place, and he wasn't going to let anyone invade it.

One of the people knocked on his door, making him jump. He shouldn't have been surprised. He'd seen them coming. It was why he set the obstacle in front of the door.

"Are you ready?" Eric asked.

No. But was that going to stop them? He couldn't live with himself knowing Allie had to go to the saloon because he wouldn't marry her. With a sigh, he called out, "Yes, I'm ready."

"Are you going to come out here?" Caroline asked.

Travis couldn't believe his ears. Why did she think he had Eric lug all of his things out to this building? "No, I'm staying in here."

"You are?" Caroline replied, sounding incredulous.

Thankfully, the judge interjected at this point. "We can do it this way. All Travis and Allie have to do is agree to the vows. They don't need to see each other."

Which was for the best.

The judge cleared his throat. "We are gathered here today to join in holy matrimony Travis Martin and Allison Jones. Marriage is an honorable institution and not to be entered into lightly."

Travis snorted. What irony. This whole thing was being done with very little thought or care.

The judge paused, indicating that everyone on the other side had heard him, and Travis' body warmed with embarrassment.

Clearing his throat, Travis said, "Pardon me. I sneezed." Fine. So it was a lie. But did everyone really want to know the truth?

"As I was saying," the judge picked back up, "this is an honorable institution in the sight of God and man. If anyone wants to back out of this, now's the time to do it. Once the vows are said, there's no undoing them."

The judge waited, but as Travis expected, no one thought it best to warn the poor woman she'd be better off joining a convent than strapping herself to the likes of him. He didn't even know if that was possible at this point. Probably not. She'd made the trip here, and she probably didn't have the money to go to one. He would've offered to pay it, but he had no more than what he owned on the property, which wasn't worth much. So…marriage it was.

"Alright," the judge said. "Since no one voiced any objections, I'll go right on with it. Travis, do you take Allison Jones to be your wife? Do you promise to love, honor, and protect her all the days of your life? Will you keep her in sickness and in health, for richer or poorer, for better or worse, forsaking all others for as long as you both shall live?"

Wincing, Travis forced out, "I do."

The judge repeated the same vows to her, and something in Travis hoped she might say no and save them both the misery, but, in a soft voice he could barely hear, she said yes. Well, that did it. Now their fates were sealed. The poor woman. From this point on, her life would be miserable.

"By the power vested in me," the judge continued, "I now pronounce you husband and wife. Under ordinary circumstances, I'd say you could kiss the bride, but I see no point since you're behind a door."

Travis wanted to tell Allie he was sorry, that if it'd been up to him, she would have found someone better, but the words died in his throat when Caroline congratulated the two of them.

Since everyone was distracted by listening to Caroline go on and on about how wonderful marriage was and how much she looked forward to getting to know Allie better, Travis dared a peak through the small window by the door. Caroline was hugging Allie, so he didn't get a good look at her until Caroline let go of her.

Even from a distance, he knew Allie was pretty. But what he had failed to realize was just *how* beautiful she was. She didn't have a single blemish on her smooth, pale skin. No scars tarnished her appeal. Plus, she was perfectly proportioned. She had a nice hourglass figure. Indeed, she seemed more like an artist's dream than a real woman.

He shook his head and slipped away from the window. A couple couldn't be more mismatched. What was she doing with someone like him? If she'd been ugly…if she'd had some deformity, this might not be such a horrible ordeal. Or even if she had an ordinary appearance, it might be bearable. But she was the most beautiful woman he'd ever seen. And she was stuck with him. A feeling of unease welled up in his gut. He'd just condemned that poor woman to a lifetime with him. Just how was he supposed to make it up to her? He couldn't. He could spend his entire life giving her gifts and apologizing, and it'd never be enough.

***

Eric and Caroline gave Allie some food a woman named Lois had made for her before they left with the judge. Caroline had promised she'd come out the next day with a friend. Allie didn't recall the friend's name. Nor did she care to at the moment.

She was all alone out here with a man known to frighten most of the people in town. A man, as it turned out, who refused to show her his face. She shivered. Maybe the whole thing shouldn't have spooked her, but it did.

She spent the rest of the day cleaning. There was so much to clean, she wasn't sure where to start, but in the end, she figured the kitchen would be the best place since she'd be cooking food in here. Fortunately, there was a covered barrel of fresh water by the door. She made haste to grab enough for the pitcher and a bucket before she hurried to lock the door.

After that, she occupied her time with cleaning the best she could. In the dim light coming through the parted curtains, it was hard to tell if she was doing a good job. But the water in the bucket was quickly becoming a murky brown, so she figured the kitchen had to be better off than it had been.

One thing she did like about the shade from the trees was that it made the cottage cooler than it would've been otherwise. The wind drifting in from the open windows also helped. So the task turned out to be less daunting than she had feared when she started.

At one point, she heard some pounding coming from the large building. She stopped scrubbing the floor and went to the kitchen window. The window of the building was open, but the cottage was too far from the building for her to get a good view of what was happening in there.

Her mind unwittingly went back to the warning the judge had given her. Was Travis working on some gruesome project? Just what kind of things did a man with his reputation work on? He was so secretive. The only way she was going to find out what he was doing was to sneak up to the building and peek into that window. But she didn't dare.

It was best she didn't know. She didn't need to get caught up in whatever horrible activity he was doing. Swallowing the lump in her throat, she turned back to the floor and continued scrubbing it.

By the time she was done, it was late. The sun was setting for the day, and the flame in the kerosene lamp was pretty much the only source of light she had left. Her body aching, she stretched, working out the kinks in her muscles. She scanned the room, noting that while the room looked better, there was still a long way to go.

Deciding she'd dump out the dirty water tomorrow when the sun was back out, she ate a quiet and quick meal at the window. She watched the building. As far as she could tell, Travis hadn't lit a candle or a lamp. The place remained dark. Maybe he didn't need a light. Maybe he could see in the dark.

When she was done eating, she closed all the windows, locked them, and made sure the door was still locked. Feeling only a little bit better, she took the kerosene lamp and went to the bedroom. The place looked even more foreboding in the evening than it had in the day, something she didn't think possible.

She set the lamp on the dresser, acutely aware of the missing mirror. Not sure what she'd find in the drawers, she pulled them out and saw they were free of dust. Probably because Travis had put his clothes in them. Well, she might as well do the same with her things.

She thought the process would go smoothly because she had turned the wick up all the way for maximum lighting. But while she was putting one of her shirtwaists away, she thought she heard a noise from the other room.

She stilled and listened. She didn't hear anything else, but that did little to comfort her. Gripping the shirtwaist, she debated whether or not she should investigate the cottage. If she didn't, she might not be able to sleep. She put the shirtwaist away and then straightened up.

After she took a deep breath, she reached out for the kerosene lamp, noting the way her hand trembled. She quickly put her other hand under the base to support it, lest she drop it and squash out the only source of light she had, and slowly made her way to the door.

This was so different than how she'd imagined her wedding night would be. She knew things would be awkward, but she'd thought her husband would be a normal human being and would want to spend time with her. She hadn't expected this scenario in a million years.

Well, whether she'd expected it or not didn't change things. This was going to be her life, for better or worse. And as she stood in the doorway, her gaze going across the shadows in the parlor, it was looking like it was going to be worse.

She took a tentative step forward, her gaze seeking out all the corners in the room. Nothing struck her as unusual. Everything looked like it had earlier. So far, so good. She waited for any other suspicious sounds, but all was quiet.

She proceeded further into the parlor, and after being assured nothing was going to jump out and attack her, she went to the other bedroom since it was closer to her than the kitchen. A careful search didn't give her anything to worry about there, either.

That left the kitchen. The kitchen was where the door was. Bracing herself, she tiptoed to the kitchen, listening for anything she should worry about. All was quiet. And while that probably should have been reassuring, it only spooked her all the more.

She tiptoed to the kitchen, holding her breath the entire way. Once she was at the threshold, she peeked into the room. Nothing seemed out of place. The room was just as sparse as the other rooms. She didn't think anyone could easily hide here.

As she inspected the small area, she saw that the brush she'd been using had fallen off the table and had landed on the floor. She started to laugh then, and with the laughter came some tears that found their way down her cheeks. She'd never been more relieved to see a brush in her entire life.

She returned to the bedroom and put the kerosene lamp on the dresser. Wiping her eyes, she closed the door and scooted her trunk in front of it. There. Just in case someone—Travis or otherwise—did come in, she'd have enough warning. The trunk might only be halfway full, but it was still heavy enough to make the person work in order to push it aside. She'd finish emptying it later.

She looked at the bed, wondering if she really wanted to lie down in it. Caroline had taken the time to pull up the blankets and fluff the pillow in an attempt to make things more comfortable for her, but Allie didn't know if she could get comfortable in something Travis slept in. With all the rumors circulating about him, wasn't it possible his blanket and pillow might have some creepy crawly things living in them?

After a long moment, she pulled back the blanket and studied it and the sheet underneath. She then inspected the pillow. They looked alright. She brought the pillow up to her nose. It didn't smell bad. It didn't smell terrific, either, but at least there was no foul odor coming from it. She then smelled the blanket and sheet. Again, everything smelled fine. Feeling a bit safer, she lifted the sheet and checked the straw mattress. That looked alright, too.

Relieved, she settled into the bed. Though she was warm because she had closed and locked the window before she pulled the dusty curtains over it, she refused to get undressed. If she needed to get up in the middle of the night, for whatever reason, she wanted to be prepared.

So she pulled back the blanket and settled onto the bed. She was about to drift off to sleep when an image crept into her mind. It was the image of a man covered with hair. He had three eyes and long fingernails. He was hovering over her, as if ready to devour her. Gasping, she bolted up into a sitting position.

No monster was in the room with her. She was safe. She was alone. All was quiet in the house. Wiping the sweat from her brow, she fluffed the pillow again. Since the head of the bed was against the wall, she propped the pillow up along the wall and rested her back on it.

She was too awake now to drift off to sleep. And worse, there was nothing she could do to pass the time. She didn't dare clean anything while it was too dark to see what was outside. If she'd had the room in her trunk, she would have brought a couple of books to read, but since there hadn't been room, she'd only packed what was necessary.

That left her with nothing to do but wait for morning. And that meant she had to go through a very long and stressful night. She had a pocket watch, but she decided not to look at it. She didn't need to watch each minute ticking away, each tick going slower than the last. It was bad enough she could feel how slow time was passing.

There were a couple times during the night her head fell forward and she was able to drift off to sleep, but these moments were short in duration. She'd jerk awake and be searching out the room, her gaze going to the doorknob to make sure no one was trying to come in.

By the time she noticed the sliver of light coming in through a part in the curtains, she jumped off the bed and opened them. She released her breath and nearly cried with relief. It was finally dawn. Still not feeling secure enough to part the curtains, she pulled them back together then returned to bed, this time lying down. It took a while, but she was finally able to go to sleep.

Chapter Four

Travis wasn't usually an early riser, but that morning, he woke right after dawn. He sat up in the makeshift bed he'd made out of some boards and old drapes Lois hadn't wanted anymore. The bed was uncomfortable, of course, and he was so tall, his feet dangled off the edge, but it'd worked well enough.

What he ought to do was get some hay from the barn loft and stuff the drapes with it. Then he could sew them and give himself some cushion for this night. Sooner or later, he'd need to make himself a good mattress, but for now, this would work. As far as he was concerned, Eric owed him the materials for a good mattress after manipulating him into marriage.

He rose to his feet and lumbered to the window. From this angle, he couldn't see much of the cottage, but he did see that the kitchen window was covered with the curtains. It was also closed. The door was partially obstructed with a tree, but it was closed as well.

Good. That worked to his advantage. Maybe he could get some work done outside without being seen. The hour was still early, and Allie had had a long day yesterday, what with coming into town off the stagecoach. If he was going to do anything outside, he needed to do it now.

Careful not to make too much noise, he quickly got dressed then left the building. After he took care of the animals, he gathered enough straw for the bed and lugged that into the building. From there, he grabbed a basket and gathered ripe fruit from the trees and pulled up ripe vegetables from the garden. Allie would have some of the breads and muffins Lois had had Eric deliver to him a couple days ago.

Travis put a couple of fruits and vegetables on the small table next to his bed then took the breadbox off the shelf. He opened it and removed a loaf of bread. He usually had snacks while out here. But now this is where he'd eat all the time. When Eric came out, he'd make sure to give Eric a list of items to buy for him and Allie at the general store.

Later today or maybe tomorrow, he'd have to check his traps and see if he'd caught any fresh meat. Hopefully, he had. Allie would probably like a variety of food.

After he ate, he pulled on a cloak, securing it around his head to hide his face, and carried the basket to the front door of the cottage. He set the basket down and hurried on back to the building, hoping she hadn't heard him. He was a large man. Who knew if his footsteps boomed when he walked?

Once he was safely back in the building, he released his breath, unaware he'd been holding it. His heart was beating so fast he thought it might jump out of his chest. He had no idea having someone else on his property, especially someone as pretty as Allie, was going to have this effect on him.

Now whenever he left the safety of his building, he was going to have to worry she'd see him. Even with the cloak, he felt exposed. He never should have agreed to marry her. He should have insisted Eric either take her in and give her a suitable job or take her to Carl Richie to marry.

In haste, he'd made the decision to marry her, and he was going to live with that mistake for the rest of his life. He groaned and sat down. The piles of cut up lumber of all shapes and sizes and other objects like metals and cloths pretty much took up one end of the building to another. He hadn't realized how crowded the place was until this moment.

Up to now, he'd taken comfort in the things. It was from these things he made stuff people could use, and sometimes a few came to collect some of the pieces for their own projects. It'd been enough to give him a decent living. They either paid him in money or food, and he hadn't had a need to go to town.

He'd been very comfortable with this arrangement. His world had been good. Predictable. Safe. Just the way he wanted it. But in one day, all of that had changed, and he was too afraid of what the changes meant to even think about them.

He rose to his feet and gathered some lumber. There was one chair in the kitchen that was loose. He'd been meaning to fix it, but he never got around to it. He hardly ate in there, so it kept slipping his mind. Being that she was a woman, however, Allie probably would spend a lot more time in the kitchen than he ever did. And that meant she'd need good chairs.

He might not be able to change their situation, but he could make her life easier. Once he had all the lumber he needed, he gathered his tools and got to work.

***

Allie's eyes flew open, and she sat straight up in bed. Something woke her, but as she tried to figure out what it was, she didn't hear anything. That didn't mean she could lower her guard, though. She got out of the bed, lowered the wick on the lamp until the flame was out, and checked all the rooms. Nothing was unusual. The cottage was as depressing as it'd been the day before.

None of the locks had been tampered with, and that made her feel better. But only slightly. She proceeded to unlock the windows and open them. Everything was quiet. A look out at the building didn't tell her any more than it had yesterday. Travis was probably still in there.

That was good because she needed to relieve her bladder. The only place to do that was in the small wooden outhouse. Thankfully, it wasn't anywhere near the barn or building, so she didn't need to pass those on her way there.

Forcing aside her unease, she unlocked the door and opened it. She was about to take a step forward when she noticed the basket full of apples, cherries, berries, tomatoes, cucumbers, red peppers, and onions.

Surprised, she remained in the doorway for a long moment. There was only one person who would have brought this to her. Her gaze went back to the building. Was that what had woken her up? Had she heard him bring the basket to the door?

She bent down and picked it up. It was heavy. There were a lot of fruits and vegetables in here. Probably enough to last her a couple weeks. With another glance at the building, she brought the basket into the kitchen and set it on the table. She picked up one of the apples and inspected it. Then she chose to inspect a cucumber. If the rest of the basket's contents were in as good condition as the apple and cucumber, then it told her something important about her new husband.

Unlike the condition of his property which required a fresh coat of paint and tidying up, he was careful with his food. He even laid out the food so it was attractive to the eye. She couldn't help but note the appeal in the arrangement, especially with the assortment of colors. Surely, a man who took such care in doing this and bringing it to her door couldn't be as bad as she'd originally feared.

After a moment, she decided she had to relieve her bladder or else she'd be dealing with a mess she'd rather not clean up. So she left the cottage and found the outhouse close by. The anxiety she'd had earlier was partially replaced with a new curiosity.

Just what did that basket mean? Did it mean he wanted to talk to her? Did it mean he wanted to learn about her? Not everyone could write. Maybe the only way he could get a message to her was by sending her things like that basket. So maybe it was up to her to reply.

Once she took care of her needs and brushed her hair to make herself more presentable, she decided to go to the building. The sunlight helped immensely in calming her nerves. There was still a spark of the fear she'd experienced all through the night, but in the day, it was easier to push those fears to the back of her mind. And despite her restless night's sleep, she did feel better about everything this morning. Things often looked better after sleep, anyway. So maybe that was it.

She stopped in front of the building, and taking a deep breath, she knocked on the door.

She couldn't be sure, but she thought she heard something fall to the floor. A long moment passed with no sound from the other side of the door. No one called out to her. No one approached the door. Biting her lower lip, she knocked a second time, making sure she did it louder so he had to hear her. But again, there was no response.

She thought about calling out to him, but a cool breeze swept across her, giving her a chill, so she thought better of it. Maybe this wasn't a good idea after all. Maybe she was better off staying in the cottage. Or at the very least, she should stay to her side of the property.

She retreated back to the cottage and went inside. With a glance at the building, she saw it was just as it had been before. No one seemed to be in there, though she knew full well there was.

Her gaze went back to the basket where everything had been carefully laid out in a beautiful display. Just what kind of man had she married? Was he a monster, or was he a man who possessed an eye for beauty? She didn't know what to think.

Well, either way, she supposed it didn't matter at the moment. Right now, she had work to tend to. This cottage wasn't going to clean itself. Picking up the bucket from yesterday, she dumped out the dirty water, cleaned it out at the well, and filled up it up with clean water.

Then she returned to the house with it, only pausing once to glance at the building. This time she saw someone moving around inside. But the image was only there for a second. She hurried back into the cottage and started to work.

***

It wasn't until around nine when someone knocked on the cottage door. Allie had been so focused on wiping down the parlor walls that she almost fell off the chair. Was it him? Had Travis come over?

There was another knock followed by a female voice asking, "Allie, are you there?"

Relaxing, Allie stepped down from her chair and put the rag in the soapy bucket. She hurried to the door, excited by the prospect of talking to someone after the long night and morning by herself.

She'd thought for sure she wouldn't want to see Caroline for a long time, given that it was Caroline and Eric's idea to marry her to Travis. But the time alone had eased her disappointment over the new change of plans.

She opened the door and saw Caroline, Caleb, and another woman.

"How are you doing today, Allie?" Caroline asked.

"Alright," Allie replied. *All things considered.* She gestured for them to enter. "Come on in."

"Thank you," Caroline went in with Caleb, followed by the new woman. "This is my friend, Phoebe Thomas. She's married to Abe."

"It's nice to meet you," Phoebe told her.

"It's nice to meet you, too," Allie replied.

"We came to help you clean this place," Caroline said.

"Oh, you don't have to do that," Allie protested.

"Nonsense," Caroline argued. "We want to. It's the least I can do after taking the gentleman you were supposed to marry."

Noting the sincerity in Caroline's voice, Allie smiled. "I was delayed, and the mail didn't go out right away when I was in Missouri. I'm sure Eric didn't think I was still coming."

"No, he didn't. I had a friend who was supposed to marry a gentleman, but she fell in love while traveling on the train and married another one instead. Sometimes people never make it to their destination."

"And sometimes a woman thinks she's going to marry someone who wasn't expecting her," Phoebe added. "A man wrote a mail-order bride ad pretending to be Abe."

Allie's eyes grew wide. "No!"

Phoebe nodded. "He was Carl Richie."

"So, that's why you married Abe?" Allie asked.

"Abe wasn't all that excited to marry me at first," Phoebe replied, "but it worked out."

"And what about Carl Richie?" Allie asked. "Why did he do such a thing?" It seemed like a horrible thing to do to an innocent woman.

"It's a long story," Phoebe began, "but suffice it to say that Carl thought if Abe got married, he would be so preoccupied with his wife that he'd forget about the stream and land their father left Carl in the will."

"That's awful," Allie said. "You were nothing but a pawn."

"It seems like it's all going to work out anyway," Phoebe assured her. "Carl's wife is dead now, and he has no children. The will stipulated that if he doesn't have a child by the time he's thirty, Abe gets the stream and the land around it."

"My husband is still looking for the person who killed Carl's wife," Caroline inserted. "He has a list of suspects, but until he has proof, he can't do anything."

Allie glanced from one woman to another, thinking this story sounded stranger than her marriage to Travis did. Maybe she wasn't as bad off as she'd thought.

"Caleb," Caroline said, turning to the boy, "why don't you go see Travis? We have a lot to talk about, and it'll only bore you."

Caleb nodded then headed for the building. Allie watched him as he went to the door. He wasn't the least bit afraid of Travis. In fact, his steps were certain, as if he wanted to go there. He knocked on the door, and after a moment, the door opened. Allie strained to get a glimpse of the man she'd just married, but all she could make out was a tall silhouette before Caleb slipped into the building. The door closed behind him, successfully removing any other glimpse she might get of Travis.

"Have you seen Travis yet?" Caroline asked her.

Allie shook her head. "Not yet." Then her gaze went to Phoebe. "Have you seen him?"

"Only a little bit," Phoebe said. "He had his hat low over his eyes. I couldn't make out much more than his mouth and chin."

"I've seen his entire face, and he looks like a normal man. Well, except for the scars."

"Abe said he got those scars from a childhood bout of varicella," Phoebe said. "Travis once told him he couldn't stop scratching, and it was the scratching that left the scars."

"Really?" Caroline asked, surprised. "I didn't know that."

"It's not something Travis talks about," Phoebe replied. "He's terribly self-conscious about his face because of it."

"Does he know about the rumors in town?" Allie asked.

Caroline let out a frustrated sigh. "I really wish people would stop such nonsense. Travis is not the monster they make him out to be. Why, would I trust my child to see him if he was?"

Caroline had a good point. There was no denying that. If Caroline had thought there was anything to the rumors, she would have at least gone into the building with him.

"We can talk more while we help you clean," Caroline said.

"Yes," Phoebe agreed. "I can see this place needs a lot of work, and it'll go faster if we do it together."

Allie smiled at them. "I do appreciate the help. I admit that I was overwhelmed when I first saw how dirty it was."

Phoebe returned her smile. "Men don't see things the way women do. As long as a rodent or bug isn't somewhere, they figure it's clean."

Allie shuddered. Good heavens, but she hadn't thought about rodents!

"I'll get fresh water," Caroline said as she picked up the bucket.

"And I'll start the laundry," Phoebe added, picking up a washboard and large metal tub.

That left Allie with cleaning more walls. Thanking them for their help, she hurried to continue with the chores.

Chapter Five

Travis watched the flurry of activity around the cottage as Caroline and Phoebe went to the well.

"You don't need to be scared," Caleb said from behind him.

Turning from the edge of the window, Travis looked at the boy, who seemed to be able to see him despite the hat he'd carefully pulled low over his forehead.

"They want to help," Caleb added then went over to the chair Travis had been working on. "You're almost done."

Though Travis wasn't used to children, he saw no harm in talking to this one. Caleb was just as different from the others in town as he was, except Caleb didn't have a face and body marked with scars. He only had dark skin. The others in town, Travis included, had white skin. There was one exception. Abe Thomas was half-Cherokee and half-white. But Caleb was black.

And that would make him stand out. Just as Travis and Abe stood out. It was an unfortunate thing since people had so much trouble accepting those different from them. The last thing Caleb needed was more people treating him like an outcast. He needed someone who could accept him as he was, and Travis could be one of those few people who wouldn't make him feel unwelcome in this town.

He went over to the chair, noting the way Caleb ran his hand down the rough edges. "I'm only halfway done. I haven't sanded out the rougher parts or painted it yet," he said.

Caleb glanced up at him. "What does sanding do?"

"It makes the wood smooth." He retrieved two pieces of sandpaper and handed one to him. "This is how you do it." He ran the paper along one of the legs, and bits of the rough part of the wood fell to the floor. "Don't mind the mess. That's normal. I just sweep it when I'm done." He stopped sanding and ran his fingers along the leg. "That's smooth. Want to feel it?"

Caleb nodded, so Travis moved aside. Caleb touched the smooth wood and then brought his hand back to a rough section. "I like the difference."

"One of the nice things about making something with your hands is that you get to see it evolve," Travis replied as he continued sanding the leg. "You can turn junk into something people can use, like a chair." He gestured to the pile of junk around him. "This is all junk people threw away."

"Do they bring it here?" Caleb asked then started smoothing the top of the chair.

"No. Well, some do. Usually, your pa will collect junk and bring it out here to see if I can use any of it. There are a couple of other men who bring things by. But most of the time, I go to the place where people dump their garbage."

"Where's that?"

"It's a small area outside of town. There's a big hole dug out there, and most people will throw their junk in there. Sometimes, however, the object is too big, so they put it in a row with other large objects."

"What kind of objects do people throw away?"

"Believe it or not, I've found a couple of good wagons out there."

"I don't understand," Caleb said, his eyebrows furrowed. "If the wagons are good, why do they throw them away?"

"Because they don't realize those wagons are still good. There might be some rotted wood or wheels that don't work right, but overall, it can be fixed. I take those and fix them. Your pa is good about taking them and selling them for me. I let him keep a portion of the money for his help."

"You like my pa, don't you?"

Travis hesitated to express his feelings. He wasn't used to doing it. It was easier to deal with things than it was to deal with emotions, but there was a thoughtful expression on the child's face that prompted him to open up to him. He couldn't be sure what it was, but it seemed that the boy had a way of understanding things that most people didn't.

"To be honest," Travis began, "your pa is one of the few people I trust in this town. He's a good man." After a moment, he added, "I consider him to be a friend."

"He likes you, too," Caleb replied. "He doesn't think it's right when people say the things they do about you."

Travis stopped sanding the leg and watched as Caleb continued to work as if he hadn't just exposed something of significance. But who knew? Caleb might be perceptive, but he was still a child. Maybe he didn't realize how much the rumors bothered Travis. Maybe he assumed since Travis was an adult, he didn't have feelings like children did.

"You can't help what people say about you, Caleb. I learned that a long time ago. The important thing is to believe in yourself. You're a smart boy. Smarter than most, I'm guessing."

Caleb took a moment to look over at him, those eyes suggesting he was mature for his age. "Do you believe in yourself?"

The question shouldn't have shocked him. He did, after all, just get through telling Caleb to believe in himself. It was natural Caleb would want to know if Travis was following his own advice. But the truth was, it was much easier to tell someone else to believe in himself than to do it. And he didn't know how to explain that to Caleb without sounding weak.

"I believe in the work I do," Travis finally said, hoping it was a good enough answer.

Fortunately, Caleb seemed content with it and resumed his work on the chair. Relieved, Travis started sanding another leg.

***

"I can't believe this is the same room you were cleaning when we got here," Caroline told Allie as the two inspected the parlor around one o'clock.

Allie's gaze swept the clean hardwood floor, the newly scrubbed walls, the white curtains which had been washed and hung to dry, and the dust-free sofa, rocking chair, and table. "It looks like it belongs in a different house."

"Nope. It all belongs here."

Allie wouldn't have believed this possible when she came here yesterday. But seeing this room as it was intended to be gave her a flicker of hope that maybe—just maybe—everything was going to be alright after all.

"Lunch is ready," Phoebe said as she came into the room. "Although it's later than I expected. It took me time to find all the ingredients I needed." She inspected the parlor. "You two are finished already?"

"There was nothing to it," Caroline replied with a big grin. "I took one task, Allie took another, and here it is!"

Phoebe put her hand up to her chest and laughed. "My goodness. I wouldn't have thought this possible this morning."

"Me neither," Allie admitted.

"Just you wait until we get to the bedrooms tomorrow," Caroline told her. "Then you'll have a whole new home." Her eyes grew wide. "That reminds me. Eric and I got you a new sheet, pillow, and blanket for the bed."

"What?" Allie asked, surprised. "You didn't have to do that."

"We wanted to. It's a gift. You know, for all the trouble we caused you." Caroline offered her a smile. "It's the least we can do."

Allie didn't know how to respond to that, so she could only watch as Caroline hurried out of the cottage.

With a chuckle, Phoebe turned to Allie. "She has a good heart. She feels bad that she stole your husband."

Allie laughed. "Well, to be fair, I wasn't married to Eric when she came here."

"Yes, but she married him before you could. She got off in this town by mistake. She was supposed to marry a man further out west."

"She was?"

"Yes, but it turned out to be a very good thing she didn't. The man she was supposed to marry wanted to sell her into prostitution."

Allie gasped. "He what?"

"I know," Phoebe said with a shiver. "Being a mail-order bride myself, it scares me to think of how vulnerable we all were when we answered those ads. You can't tell much about a man through written correspondence."

"No, I suppose you can't." In light of this, Allie was glad she'd been delayed so that Caroline had to marry Eric. She would hate to think of any woman ending up with such a terrible life. "I'm glad she ended up with Eric."

"Travis is a good man, too," Phoebe quickly said, as if she thought Allie needed the assurance. "Sometimes things don't turn out the way we expect, but that doesn't mean we aren't exactly where we're meant to be."

Since Allie didn't know how to answer that, she settled for nodding. Maybe Phoebe was right. Maybe she wasn't. Either way, Allie didn't know Travis well enough to make a decision about it.

"Do you mind if I ask you what you think of Travis?" Phoebe asked.

Allie shrugged. "I don't know what to think. I haven't seen him, and we haven't had a single conversation. There was a door between us when we said our vows. He seems more like a shadow than an actual person."

Phoebe smiled. "Travis is so terribly shy. Abe says the prettier the woman, the shier he is. You're more beautiful than me or Caroline, and he hides whenever we're around. But if Abe says he'll make a good husband, you can bet on it."

Caroline came back into the cottage, saving Allie from having to reply. "You'll never believe what Travis is making for you, Allie," Caroline said as she came into the room, a neatly folded blanket, sheet, and a pillow in her arms. "Caleb said he's making a chair for you," she added, glancing over at Caleb as he came into the room behind her. "Caleb has been helping him sand and paint it."

"Did Travis say why he's making a chair for Allie?" Phoebe asked, directing her question to Caleb.

"One of the kitchen chairs is wobbly," Caleb replied.

Was it? Allie went to the kitchen chairs and tested them. Sure enough, one wasn't sturdy. Maybe he saw no use in making any new chairs before since he'd been alone out here. Maybe he didn't make it a habit of entertaining people.

"Does he have visitors?" Allie asked as Caroline and Phoebe came into the kitchen.

"From what Abe said, he doesn't visit with people," Phoebe told her. "He's never invited Abe inside this cottage. Abe's only seen that building where he makes things." Though unnecessary, she gestured toward it. "He and Abe say whatever they need to in there, and then Abe leaves. He never stays for longer than a few minutes."

"Eric does the same thing," Caroline added.

Then it made sense why he never bothered to do anything about the wobbly chair or anything else in the little home.

"Now that you're here," Caroline continued, "we have a reason to come out and visit. Of course, that's only if you'd like us to. We don't want to impose. If you'd rather not have us around, you don't have to. There's nothing worse than feeling like you have to be social when you don't feel like it."

"Right," Phoebe added, directing Allie's gaze to her. "We only want to come over if you want us here."

Allie returned their smiles. "I'd love it if you came to visit."

She noted the relief on Caroline's face and suspected Caroline understood she no longer held any hard feelings for the way things had turned out.

"We'll have to show you where we live," Phoebe said. "That way you can come over and visit us if you wish."

"Thank you," Allie replied.

It was nice to know she wasn't alone in this town, and she sensed that these two women could become good friends. While Caroline went to change the bedding in Allie's bedroom, Phoebe helped Allie with lunch.

***

"I'm surprised you bothered showing your face around here," Hank called out as Carl Richie entered the general store.

Carl glanced over his shoulder as the old man followed him into the place. "I have nothing to hide," Carl told him. "I didn't kill my wife."

"We can't be sure about that," Daniel said from behind him.

Carl spun around and saw that Daniel was with two other men: Mike and Jerry. "The sheriff says I'm *not guilty*," he replied. "And besides, why would I kill her? I need a legitimate child before I turn thirty." Speaking of which… He looked directly at Daniel. "Did I get any mail?"

"Yeah, let me get it," Daniel said then lumbered over to the post office, which was in the store.

"I don't know," Hank commented, crossing his arms and scanning Carl up and down as if he'd find traces of Lydia's blood somewhere on his clothes. "You had a lot more to gain by getting rid of her than keeping her alive."

"Yeah," Jerry agreed, "and you were awfully quick to post an ad for a mail-order bride. Someone might think there's something suspicious about that."

Carl rolled his eyes. "I need a child by the time I'm thirty. That's only eighteen months away."

"If you were in that much of a hurry, why didn't you marry Miss Allison Jones when she came into town yesterday?" Hank asked.

"I didn't even know there was a Miss Allison Jones in town," Carl replied.

Carl almost added, *Who is Allison Jones*? But he refrained. The men had all marked him down as being guilty of Lydia's murder, even though he hadn't done it. For all he knew, one of them could have been the killer. He had no idea who would have done the deed, but there were plenty of motives to go around. Lydia often said she knew enough secrets about people in town that she could get whatever she wanted. Maybe she'd been blackmailing someone.

"I got mail for you," Daniel said, coming up to him.

Carl turned from the men and accepted the envelope. The script was definitely feminine. Maybe this one would be the answer to his prayers. The other one sure hadn't been.

"I hope you don't leave town," Jerry spoke up.

"Yeah," Mike said. "We might need you here. Just in case the sheriff's wrong."

"The sheriff isn't infallible," Jerry agreed.

Carl glanced from one accusing stare to another. This town hadn't been the friendliest one to begin with, but now, everyone had turned on him because they all assumed he was guilty. Just because he hated Lydia, it didn't mean he killed her. Sure, he'd often fantasized about her death, but he'd never tried to kill her.

"When the real killer is exposed, and he will be, I'll be waiting for all of your apologies," Carl finally snapped.

Hank snorted.

"Especially from you since you made it a habit of sleeping with Lydia," Carl told Hank. "You will be the first in line to apologize."

"That'll be the day," Hank retorted.

"Hands and knees." Carl pointed to the ground. "You will have to get on your hands and knees if you expect me to forgive you."

As Carl stormed out of the store, Hank yelled out, "If you could have satisfied her in bed, she wouldn't have kept coming to mine to get the job done right."

Gritting his teeth, Carl ignored him as he slipped the letter into his pocket. He made haste in unhitching the horse from the post and jumped into the saddle. Then he rode off as fast as the horse would take him, ignoring the dirty looks and shouts from the people who were covered in dust as the horse stirred it up into the air.

What did he care? None of the people liked him. They had nothing but contempt for him. Always had. Always would.

He hated this place. From the moment he was a child and his father brought him and his mother here, he'd hated this place. It had lacked all the comforts and graces of the East.

It's only temporary, his father had told them. *I heard from a reliable source this area is ripe with gold. In a little while, we'll go back to Boston, and we'll be rich beyond our wildest dreams.*

Like a fool, Carl and his mother had believed him. But year after year had passed, and Carl was no closer to getting out of here than he had been the day he first arrived. He suspected he was close to finally finding the gold. He'd actually panned a couple of flakes the other day. For the first time in years, he had hope. Finally, there was a silver lining beginning to emerge from all the years of sorrow and despair that had hovered over his life.

He pulled the horse to a stop once he was on the outskirts of town and grabbed the letter. He ripped the envelope open and read through the missive. As he'd hoped, it was from a woman. She took time to describe herself, but he scanned down the paper to make sure his one requirement was met. She had to be a virgin. There was no way he was going to risk marrying a woman who knew how inadequate he was in bed. It was enough Lydia had known it. He didn't need the next wife mocking him, too.

The last reply he'd received was from a widow. That had been no good. He'd had to dismiss her. Though why she had bothered replying when he'd specifically mentioned wanting a virgin was still a mystery to him. Didn't these women take the time to actually read the ad he posted?

But he was in luck with this one. Her name was Juliet, and she had done a good job in making sure she met all of his requirements. Good. Yes, this one would do. He'd pen a reply, and he'd deliver it to the stagecoach driver himself when he came by in a couple weeks. He didn't trust any of the men in town to do it for him. If they all thought he was a murderer, who knew what they'd do to sabotage his chances of finally getting out of this pit of endless despair?

He put the missive back into the envelope then carefully tucked it into his pocket. For the moment, this letter was as good as the gold he hoped to soon find on his property. Feeling calmer, he urged the horse forward and took the rest of the path up to his cabin. Things were finally going in his favor.

Chapter Six

Travis didn't think Caroline, Phoebe, or Caleb would ever leave. In fact, it was half past four when they finally got into the wagon and headed on out. His father used to say women could talk for hours and hours, and darned if his father hadn't been right. He wondered if they would make it a habit of coming to the cottage now that Allie was there. Was this kind of thing going to be a frequent occurrence? And if so, what could he do about it?

He had spent the entire day getting the chair done, and now that he was finishing up with the paint, he realized the other chairs in the cottage would be eyesores next to this one. So he had no choice. He'd have to make more chairs. Considering Caroline would be bringing Caleb and Phoebe with her when she came for visits, he'd better make three others.

He honestly didn't mind Caleb. Caleb was a child, and children were far easier to talk to than adults were. They didn't judge a person before giving them a chance. They started from a place of trust and acceptance and moved from there. Adults, however, did things the other way. One had to prove they were worthy before gaining such acceptance. And Travis wasn't considered worthy.

A sound from the door interrupted his thoughts. He hid in the shadows so Allie couldn't see him and moved to the window, making sure he only peeked out the side. For the life of him, he couldn't imagine what she'd want with him. He had nothing to offer her.

He saw her bend down with something and then straighten up. Whatever had been in her hands wasn't there anymore. His eyebrows furrowed. What was she doing?

Her gaze went to the window. Gasping, he ducked, praying she hadn't noticed him. He waited for ten very long and—very tense—seconds before he dared another peek out the window. She was going back to the cottage.

He breathed a sigh of relief. That was close. Much too close.

She opened the door and slipped back into the cottage, closing it softly behind her. The trees cast enough of a shadow over the cottage for him to see her as she moved around the place.

He tried to find out what she left at the doorstep by getting another vantage point from the window, but it was no good. He couldn't see the doorstep from the window. His curiosity was prompting him to open the door to see what it was, but he didn't dare. Not right away. Not when she might be watching him from one of the windows in the cottage.

So he waited. And waited. He gave it a full half hour before he opened his door a small crack and peered down at the doorstep. It was the same basket he'd left her earlier that morning. Except, instead of fruits and vegetables, there was a covered plate and a cup with brown liquid in it.

He gave a cautious glance at the cottage. She might be watching. It was very possible. But maybe, just maybe, she'd gotten bored of waiting for him to open the door and wasn't watching. Either way, he had to know what was under the clean towel on the plate and what kind of drink was in the cup.

He lowered his hat to hide as much of his face as possible and opened the door far enough so he could retrieve the basket, careful not to upset any of the contents in it. He shut the door then tipped his hat back.

The aroma coming from the basket made his mouth water in excitement. Besides the meals Lois had made for Eric to bring out to him, he hadn't had anything warm or homemade. He brought the basket over to the workbench and lifted the cloth. Mashed potatoes, a berry cobbler, cooked carrots, and pemmican.

Surprised, he glanced back at the cottage. He didn't see her peeking out the window. Maybe she was eating. He hadn't thought she'd take the vegetables and fruits he'd brought her that morning and make him anything. He had assumed she'd fix herself meals and that would be it.

After a moment of standing around like a person who didn't know what to do with a basket full of delicious-smelling food, he finally took the basket to the other side of the building where he often ate. He placed the basket on the small table and set out each dish. He had just dug out the last dish when he realized she'd left him a note.

Curious, he lifted the neatly folded piece of paper and opened it. It was a thank you note, and more than that, she expressed her appreciation for the food and the chair he'd given her earlier that day. She added she would bring him breakfast around eight the next morning. Then, at the bottom, she had signed *Allie*.

He didn't know why such a simple thing should choke him up, but he had to blink back a few tears. Taking the note, he neatly folded it back up and took it to the small box he kept on a shelf that was tucked into the back corner of the place. The box was one he'd made when he was ten to keep important things safe.

Lifting the lid, he removed his mother's wedding ring, his father's pipe, and a small wooden train. He gently placed the note on the bottom and then put the other things on top of it. After he secured the lid, he carefully placed the box back on the shelf and returned to the table where the meal waited for him.

He pulled up a chair and sat down, not sure which of the food he should eat first. Everything looked so good. A couple minutes passed before he was able to make up his mind. He started with the carrots and mashed potatoes. He'd grown up being taught to eat his vegetables first. Then he had the pemmican since that was the meat portion of the meal, and he finished up with the berry cobbler. It all tasted as good as it looked, which made it hard to take his time and savor everything. But he managed to go slow. This was a meal fit for a king, and yet, here he was, a lowly man who had nothing of significance to his life, enjoying it.

When he was done, he washed the dishes and put them back in the basket. He retrieved a piece of paper and wrote her a note back, simply to thank her. If he'd been eloquent with words, whether in speech or in writing, he was sure he would have come up with something better. But as it was, all he could do was write out the *thank you* and leave it at that.

Once he made sure she wasn't anywhere outside, he hurried to the chicken coop and collected eggs, milked the cow, and gathered more berries. He quietly slipped around the side of the cottage, careful to crouch down low so she wouldn't see him as he passed the windows. He left the items at the door then rushed off before she could notice him. After it was dark, he went to set traps along the paths where animals were known to frequent, hoping he could provide her with meat in the future.

***

A week later, and Allie began to settle into a routine in her new life. Travis would leave her vegetables and fruits in a basket in the mornings, thanking her for her kindness toward him. On one morning, he even left fresh meat from an animal he'd skinned and prepared so that all she had to do was cook it. She, in turn, would make him meals and set them at his doorstep at the building he was staying in.

Caroline and Phoebe had helped her clean up the rest of the cottage and had taken her to town so she could get anything she needed from the general store.

Allie was surprised to learn that the store owner, Daniel, had given Travis credit since he took the old crates and other used items off his hands. In fact, Allie soon learned that a lot of people in town would give their junk to the owner who'd then take it to Travis.

Phoebe told her that Travis put all the junk he could use in the building. This led Allie to wondering what Travis did with the junk he couldn't use. Then, one evening, she noticed a fire was burning several feet from the barn. Upon investigating the matter, she saw a tower of a man burning items in a large bin. Fortunately, he hadn't seen her. He was so timid she could only imagine what he'd do if he knew she was watching him.

The next day, Lois came out with a few loaves of bread, two pies, and a plate of cookies. "I heard Travis married, and I thought by now you'd be settled in and ready to receive visitors." With a grin, she added, "I couldn't resist bringing something. I love to cook, and with it just being me, I can't eat everything I make."

"Thank you," Allie replied as she led her into the kitchen and poured them each a cup of coffee. "It's very thoughtful of you to bring me something." She gestured for Lois to sit and handed her a cup.

"I don't mind it," Lois said as Allie sat across from her. "Travis is a sweet boy. He keeps so much to himself, and he has Eric bring me money a couple times a year."

Allie stopped drinking her coffee and lowered the cup to the table. "How does he give Eric the money?"

"Eric comes out here and gets it. Eric does whatever he can to make things as easy on others as possible, and I'm sure you've noticed by now how shy Travis is."

"Yes."

Allie decided not to add that she had yet to see him. However, given how he went out of his way to make sure she had plenty of food and since he had also given her all new chairs to go around the kitchen table, she also realized he was a thoughtful person. Perhaps even more thoughtful than most.

"You really can't blame him," Lois said. "The people have made up all those horrible rumors about him. If I was him, I probably wouldn't want to show my face in town, either. There are some people who don't know when it's best to keep quiet, and sadly, you can't control what they say. You can only control how you respond to it." After a moment, she added, "I hope you don't let the rumors stop you from seeing the man he really is."

Allie wasn't sure how to answer that. But she did find Lois' words reassuring, and she found it helped her ease further into her new life. From that point on, she no longer experienced a flicker of uncertainty every time she left food at Travis' doorstep.

***

A week later, Allie was beating the rug on a clothesline to get the dust out. God only knew how long it'd been since the neatly folded rug had been used since she found it in the bottom shelf of the dresser in the second bedroom.

She swung the broom and hit the rug as hard as she could. Dust rose up and swirled around her, which, in turn, made her cough. She stepped away from the rug to get some fresh air, and as she did, she caught sight of a man riding a horse up to the property.

She didn't recognize him, and he wasn't with Caroline or Phoebe. She thought about going to the building and getting Travis, but considering how painfully shy he was, she doubted he'd answer the door. Tapping the edge of the broom, she debated whether or not she felt safe enough to deal with him herself. After a moment, she realized her gut instinct wasn't setting off any alarms. He didn't seem to pose any kind of threat. So that being the case, she walked out to meet him.

"May I help you?" she asked.

The rider pulled the horse to a stop, his eyes wide. "Does Travis Martin still live here?"

"Yes. He's in there." She pointed to the building.

He opened his mouth, as if he wanted to say something, and she guessed he was probably wondering who she was. If he knew Travis, then he must have expected Travis to be alone out here. Who knew how fast word would spread through town that she'd just married him?

"I'm Allie," she said. "I'm his wife."

"I didn't realize he was looking for a wife," the man replied. "But then, I've been too busy to worry about the latest news." He slipped off the horse. "I'm Carl Richie."

It took her a moment to realize she recognized the name. This was the man who'd posted a mail-order bride ad pretending to be someone else, and what was more, his wife had been murdered and no one knew who'd done it. She gripped the broom in her hands and took a step away from him.

Letting out a sigh, he said, "I see they already told you about me. Look, I don't want any trouble. I have a wagon that needs fixing, and I wanted to ask Travis if he'd take care of it. Right after I talk to him, I'll leave." As if to reassure her further, he added, "I promise."

She studied him for a moment then realized she believed him. Relaxing her grip on the broom, she nodded. "Travis is in the building by himself. I don't think you'll be interrupting anything."

"Thanks." Carl led the horse past her and went to the building.

As he knocked on the door and called out Travis' name, she turned her attention back to the rug. She banged more dust out of the thing, and if she was right, there was considerably less dust that swirled in the air this time.

Encouraged, she continued beating the rug, only pausing when Travis opened the door and welcomed Carl in. Again, she didn't get much of a look at Travis. No matter how hard she tried, she just couldn't get a good view of his face. If she'd been a man, she'd probably get to see him. But then, if she was a man, she wouldn't have married him. What a frustrating thing it was to not be able to see what he looked like.

By now, she'd dismissed the notion of him having three eyes or two noses or some other horrible deformity. If Carl, Eric, and Caleb had seen him and not been horrified, then the gossip about Travis had been unjustified. Not only that, but Travis struck her as a kind person. He didn't have to bring her vegetables, fruits, milk, meat, or eggs. He didn't have to clean the dishes before returning the basket to her, either. The condition of the property might leave a lot to be desired, but he was thoughtful and considerate. Those weren't traits a monster would display.

The door of the building opened, and she glanced over her shoulder. Carl shut the door behind him and got back on his horse. He called out a polite good-bye to her then trotted off the property.

This was a strange town. Travis hadn't been quite the scary man the judge would have her believe him to be. And just now, it didn't seem as if Carl was all that bad. She didn't get the gut feeling he was someone she needed to be wary of. Yes, what he'd done to Phoebe was wrong, but it was difficult to judge his motive based on the little she knew. She honestly didn't know what to think.

Well, she supposed it didn't matter what she thought one way or the other. Things were the way they were, and she couldn't do anything to change them. With a shrug, she renewed her grip on the broom and continued to beat the rug.

Chapter Seven

The next day, Carl plopped his gold panning supplies on the fallen log by the stream and rubbed his eyes. Maybe there wasn't any more than a few flakes of gold in this entire stream. Maybe all this talk of gold was a demented man's dream.

If Carl was smart, he'd accept the fact that his father was deluded and let Abe have the stream and the land that went with it. And he would have, if he had anything else worth selling so he could get out of here.

All he had was his cabin and a couple of animals. That was it. His entire life was summed up into all of this. And because of that, he had to try to find any gold that might be here. Colorado did have gold. But did this particular area have anything? The least he could do was keep going. One way or another, he had to find out.

This was the kind of debate Carl had every day he came to the stream. And, as before, the argument was enough to convince him to gather his gold pan. He slipped the classifier into it and studied the stream for a good place to dig. After a moment, he decided to focus on the area around the tree roots. Taking his digging tool and spoon, he bent down and started pulling up samples of the dirt.

He had just collected all the dirt he could fit in the pan when someone knocked into him from behind. The force of the impact threw him forward. He lost his balance, dropped the pan, and tripped over the tree roots. He landed in the stream, face first.

He barely had time to figure out what was going on when the person grabbed his hair and shoved his face into the water. And held him there, pinning him down by sitting on his back. He couldn't free himself from his attacker no matter how hard he tried.

Just when he thought his lungs were going to burst, the person brought his head up. He gasped. The air filling his lungs did little to relieve the burning sensation, but it was good to be able to take a deep breath.

But before he could enjoy it, the person brought his face back into the water and held it there. Carl had no idea how long he was under before his attacker brought his head back up.

What was the person doing? What was he trying to accomplish? If he wanted to kill him, why didn't he just hold his head under the water longer?

The next time the person lifted his head, he whispered, "Confess to the murder."

"W-what m-m-murder?" Carl gasped.

The person plunged his head back under the water. It was then Carl understood what the person referred to. Lydia's murder. Someone had killed her. It hadn't been him. He hadn't left his cabin that night. But someone had done it, and logic suggested the killer was sitting on his back, demanding he confess to the crime.

The person lifted his head again, and this time, Carl tried to look back so he could see who was on his back. But the person only forced his head back into the water. And this time, Carl hadn't taken enough of a breath to prepare for it. He inadvertently tried to breathe in the water and gagged it back up.

This time when the person lifted his head, he was too busy struggling to breathe in the air that he didn't even try to find out who was attacking him.

"Listen," the person hissed, "someone's got to take the blame. And it might as well be you. You've got nothing to live for. Out here. All alone. No family. No friends. The sheriff will go easy on you. Lydia was impossible. We all know it. You'll just spend the rest of your life in prison. Say it was an accident. Say she fought against you and fell out of the wagon. That's all you need to do. And if you don't, the next time I come for you, I won't let you live."

Then something hard hit the back of Carl's head, and everything went black.

***

Travis knocked on the door of Carl's cabin a second time and waited. There was no answer. With a sigh, Travis tipped back his hat and ran his hand through his sweaty hair. On hot days like today, he wished he could remove his hat without worrying about what others would think if they were to see him.

"You belong in the circus."

"Why don't you put a cloth over your head so we don't have to see you?"

"You look like a bear attacked you."

And on and on the snickers went from the children he'd grown up with in Eastern Colorado, and even safely out here in the mountains, he could still hear them.

Shaking his head, he forced back the memories and knocked on Carl's door a third time. "Carl? It's Travis. I came to fix your wagon."

Again, no answer.

Travis descended the porch steps and went to the barn, just to make sure Carl was still here. The saddle was still hanging on the wall, and two horses were in their stalls. It didn't look as if Carl had gone anywhere.

Then Travis remembered Carl made it a habit of panning for gold. Of course. He was probably at the stream. Travis left the barn and headed down the path that led to the gentle running water that wound through the property.

"Carl?" he called out.

The only things he heard were the water trickling over the rocks and birds chirping.

"Carl?" he called out again.

The stream was a long one, making it hard to tell whether Carl was going to be to his right or to his left. The trees lining the winding stream didn't help matters, either. With a sigh, Travis picked one direction and made his way around the trees.

It was times like this he wished he knew more about the property lines of the people around him. The last thing he wanted was to end up on someone else's land, especially someone who wasn't one of the few friendly people he'd come across in town. There were a couple who didn't take trespassers lightly. He'd heard of a man who'd been shot two years ago for trespassing on someone's land. It had turned out that the poor fellow had gotten lost.

Travis' steps slowed as he stepped into the stream so he could get a better view of his surroundings. "Carl?" he called out.

Again, no answer.

Travis glanced back in the direction he came from and decided to backtrack. If he didn't find Carl in the other direction, he'd return home and come back later.

On his way down the other way, he took a moment to kneel into the stream so he could wash his face and the back of his neck. Since no one was around to see him, he removed his hat and wet down his hair. The action did much to cool him down.

Just as he rose to his feet, something tapped his boot. Looking down, he saw a spoon used for panning gold. He retrieved it and studied the stream ahead. The sunlight streaming through the tree branches reflected off of something shiny not too far ahead.

Travis went over to it and picked up the gold pan. Along the rocks, he saw the classifier. Then, around the bend in the stream, he saw an unconscious man lying on his back. Travis ran over to the man and realized it was Carl, and he was drenched.

Wincing on Carl's behalf, Travis set the things beside him and knelt next to him. "Carl?" Travis shook his arm. "Carl, wake up."

Carl groaned.

Travis picked him up and carried him to a dry patch of grass and leaves that were far more comfortable than the stream. He tapped Carl's cheek. "Carl? I need you to wake up. Come on." He tapped his cheek again.

Carl's eyelids fluttered, and he murmured, "Where am I?"

"Along the stream."

This time, he opened his eyes, and it took him a moment to focus in on Travis.

"Are you alright?" Travis asked.

"No, no, I'm not." He sat up and rubbed the back of his head.

It was then Travis noticed the blood trickling down the back of Carl's neck. "Hold on. You're bleeding."

Carl put down his hand and inspected the blood on his fingertips while Travis ripped off a part of his shirt. "So it wasn't a dream," Carl whispered.

Travis took the fabric, searched for the wound, found it on the back of his head, and gently pressed the fabric to it. Removing the fabric, he took a good look at the actual wound. "It's not as bad as it looks," Travis told Carl. "Your head is bound to hurt, but the blood is already drying up."

"I thought for sure I was a dead man."

Now that Travis knew Carl's condition wasn't serious, he could turn his attention to how this happened to begin with. "What happened?"

"I was panning for gold, and someone came up behind me and shoved my face into the water. He said if I didn't confess to killing Lydia, he'd kill me, too."

Travis, who'd gone back to pressing the fabric over Carl's wound, shifted so he could get a good look at Carl's face. He hadn't noticed it right away, but he could see a couple of bruises on the man's face from where his face might have hit a rock or two in the stream.

The person who murdered Lydia was threatening Carl? After taking a moment to come to grips with this new piece of information, Travis asked, "Do you have any idea who attacked you?"

"No. The person was whispering. All I know is that it was a man because he was too strong to be a woman. He had me pinned in that stream," he gestured to the spot, "face first so I never saw his face."

The ramifications of this were too important to ignore. "We need to go to the sheriff. He needs to know this happened."

"I don't know."

"You don't know? Whoever did this just threatened to kill you. You have to do it."

Carl shook his head, and Travis lost his hold on the fabric. Travis picked it up, but Carl was already getting to his feet. "He was serious, Travis. It's bad enough he wants me to confess to something I didn't do. If I go to the sheriff, he'll come after me."

"It sounds like he'll come after you no matter what you do."

"Don't you think I don't know that? If he killed Lydia, there's no stopping him from killing me, too."

Travis stood up and put his hands on his hips. "Then why don't you go to the sheriff?"

"Because…because…" Carl glanced around. "I can be careful. I can set out traps along the property. It worked for Abe when Benny and Gene came for him. And I can stay in the cabin. I don't have to go to town. Maybe if I don't draw attention to myself, he'll relent."

"Or maybe you'll be an easier target." When Carl didn't respond, he added, "Even if you set out traps and stay in the cabin, he can come back here."

"But I was out in the open before."

"You can't hide here forever."

"Of course, I can. I just need to stay away from everyone else."

"But you're doing it for the wrong reason, Carl. You're letting fear keep you a prisoner here. You can't hide from the people in town forever."

"Why not? You do it."

Travis paused. Carl was right. He had let fear keep him confined to his property ever since he arrived to this town because he didn't want a repeat of what he'd gone through in the one he'd grown up in. "I have a good reason for hiding from the people in town," he said.

"And I don't?" Carl asked. "You think this lunatic threatening me is the worst of it? I'm one of the most hated people around here. Not only do most people assume I killed Lydia, but some hate me because they don't think I have a right to be on this land. This is my birthright. It's the only thing my father gave me that's worth anything. But people think I ought to just hand it on over to my father's illegitimate son even though my father purchased it, fair and square." With a shake of his head, he waved his hand in a dismissive manner. "Forget it. It doesn't matter. You have your reasons for hiding, and I have mine. In the end, does it really matter?"

Travis didn't know how to answer Carl. The man made some good points, and if Travis was going to argue them, he'd have to admit he was equally wrong for being a recluse all these years.

"You know what I want?" Carl continued. "More than anything, all I want is a fresh start. My father didn't leave me any money. All of that went to Abe's mother, and God knows what she did with it. I only have the gold in that stream. I get a little bit of gold from time to time, but so far, all I've been able to get is enough for food to get me through another year out in this godforsaken land. All I want is to be free from this place, but I can't do that without money."

Travis studied Carl, seeing a part of himself in him. Ever since he'd gotten those hideous scars, he'd put up with the taunting from the other children in town. Worse, the parents did nothing to stop it. Instead, they pitied him. His father had tried to keep him away from others as much as possible because of it, but there came a day when Travis needed to go somewhere else.

He, too, had wanted a fresh start, much like what Carl was asking now. There was the same note of desperation in Carl's voice that had once been in his. While this town was far from perfect, Travis could at least have peace here. He was out far enough where he didn't have to face anyone if he didn't want to. It wasn't like in the past where he and his father were in the center of town. He could at least go outside and not have to worry about someone seeing him.

Well, at least he hadn't until he married Allie.

"I understand what you're saying," Travis finally replied. "It's not easy when you feel like the world is against you."

Carl's face softened. "No, it's not."

"That all being said, I still think the sheriff needs to know. Even if you don't want to tell him, I'd like to. He's been looking for the murderer, and he wants to make sure he gets the right man."

"I don't know how it's going to lead the sheriff to him. The person only whispered. It's not like I have any new clues to give him."

"There might be something the sheriff will see that we're missing."

Carl crossed his arms and shifted from one foot to another. "Alright. You can tell him, but I'm not going anywhere for a while."

It wasn't what Travis had wanted to hear, but given the circumstances, he couldn't fully blame Carl. Not when he was just as guilty of hiding from others as Carl was now doing.

"Before I see the sheriff, I should at least fix your wagon," Travis said. "Why don't you go on to the cabin, and I'll collect your panning supplies?"

"Thank you," Carl replied in relief.

Travis nodded and returned to the stream.

Chapter Eight

Allie bit her thumbnail as she debated whether or not she should check out the building Travis had called home ever since she came here. Travis had left about an hour ago, and he'd taken his wagon with him. That wagon had been loaded up with tools, and a couple of new wheels. Based on what Carl Richie had told her yesterday, it didn't take a lot of guesswork to know he'd gone to Carl's place to fix his wagon.

She should have checked out the building as soon as he'd left. If she had, she'd be done by now. The only thing holding her back was the dilemma over whether or not she would be overstepping her bounds. Ever since she came here, Travis hadn't gone into the cottage. He'd confined himself to the building, only coming out to take care of the animals, to give her food, or to burn trash.

As much as she tried to get a glimpse of him, the only thing she ever saw was a silhouette. If she'd been brave enough, she would have knocked on the door of the building and stayed there until he answered it. But she wasn't that brave.

She might have been able to approach the door without worrying about him grabbing her and pulling her into the building to…to… Well, she wasn't sure what she thought he was going to do to her when she first made her afternoon treks to the building. The story of Hansel and Gretel had crossed her mind, but she reminded herself that Travis wasn't a cannibalistic witch waiting for unsuspecting people, even if a couple of the rumors in town might lead her to believe such a thing.

With a sigh, she studied the path that Travis had taken when he left. No one was on it now. In fact, it would still be too soon for him to come back. From what Phoebe said, Carl lived next to her and Abe, and it took about forty-five minutes just to get to her place from here. If Travis had only been gone for an hour, then she had about that much time left. Probably even more since fixing the wagon might take longer than thirty minutes.

Decision made, she stepped out of the cottage and hurried over to the shed, glancing at the path, just to make sure he wasn't there. She made it to the building and flung the door open. Once she was inside, she slammed it shut. Then she went to the window and scanned the path, waiting a full minute before she was convinced he wasn't there.

Backing away from the window, she released her breath. She bumped into something. Screaming, she turned around in time to see a block of wood fall off the small table she'd bumped into. Who knew something as simple as checking out what her husband was like could make her so jumpy?

She quickly picked up the block and put it back on the table. After taking a moment to regain her composure, she finally took a good look at the pile of things around her.

Just as she'd been led to believe, it was full of junk. Well, she supposed it wasn't really junk. He had made those chairs from the used lumber in here. So he took things that no one needed and made things he could use. A very practical approach, really. Having grown up without a lot, she couldn't help but appreciate his mindset on the matter.

She took in all the things he'd collected over the years. There were stacks of wood, metal, tools, and other odds and ends.

One thing she had to admit was that he was orderly. The items were all sorted and put into different sections of the large room. He'd even organized them according to size.

In the center of the room was a large table. She went over to it and saw four table legs. He'd already finished sanding three and was working on the forth one. The design matched the design he'd used for the legs on the kitchen chairs that he'd made. There was nothing wrong with the kitchen table currently in the cottage, but if he had wanted the chairs to match, then he probably also wanted the table to match.

What a peculiar man she'd married. He took great measures to hide himself from the entire world, but he was concerned with the appearance of everything he made. It almost seemed a contradiction that someone who considered himself unworthy of a mirror should be meticulous about creating something so beautiful.

And the table would be beautiful when he was done. Just the design in the legs was exquisite. There was surprising detail in them. She ran her fingers over the smooth surface.

A horse neighed, and she jerked away from the table. She rushed over to the window. If Travis caught her in here, she didn't know what she'd do. Probably die of embarrassment. He hadn't even locked the door. He'd trusted her to stay away from this building.

But when she saw Caroline and Caleb pulling up to the cottage, she relaxed. Good. It wasn't him. There was no need to find some excuse to explain why she was in here when she shouldn't have been.

She left the building and ran over to them. "Good afternoon!"

"Hi, Allie," Caroline said as she and Caleb got down from the buggy. "How are things going?"

Understanding Caroline was really wondering if things had gotten better between her and Travis, Allie said, "The same. I only catch glimpses of my husband from time to time."

Caroline frowned in disappointment, and Allie couldn't help but think Caroline was sweet for caring about her so much.

"He's been very considerate," Allie assured her. "He seems to be making me new furniture so I'll be comfortable here."

"Yes, there is that," Caroline replied. "I had just hoped that by now, he would have at least said hello." Then with a hopeful look at her, she asked, "Has he said hello?"

"Not in person, but we have corresponded a little in notes."

"Notes?"

Allie nodded. "He brings me food, and he'll thank me for the meals I make him. He even says I make the tastiest meals he's ever had. In a way, it's sweet." And it was. Allie hadn't thought about how sweet it was until she was telling Caroline about it. With a smile, she added, "I've never come across someone so shy before."

"It's a shame we don't know how he got to be as shy as he is. If we did, we might be able to help him feel comfortable enough to talk to you."

Not knowing what else to say about him, Allie decided to turn the conversation in another direction. "Would you like to come in and have something to drink? I even made some custard."

"I haven't had custard in a long time," Caroline said. She glanced at Caleb. "Have you ever had custard?"

"No," he replied.

"Then you're in for a treat," Caroline told him. Smiling at Allie, she said, "Thank you for inviting us in for refreshments. We'd love to have some."

"We both come from the South, but your ways are much more refined than mine," Allie noted as she led the two into the cottage. "How did you grow up, and what led you all the way out here?"

"Are you sure you want to know? It's a long story."

"It's so quiet out here that I'd welcome a long story."

"Since you put it that way, I'll be happy to oblige you."

Allie set out the drinks and custard as Caroline told her about her past.

***

As much as Travis hated going into town, he had to. Someone had to tell Eric what happened to Carl, and since Carl refused to do it, he was going to have to do it himself. If Lydia's murderer killed Carl, Travis wouldn't be able to handle it.

So when he finished fixing Carl's wagon, he lowered the hat over his forehead, hunched forward in the seat, and led the horses to the jailhouse. He kept his gaze forward, not daring to glance around him as the people turned to watch him. Why couldn't they ever mind their own business? Why did they always have to stop everything they were doing to stare at him? Didn't they have anything better to do?

Ignore them. Pretend they don't exist.

It was what his father used to tell him. Back then, Travis had been too young to do that, and because of that, the taunting grew worse. It took time for him to realize that ignoring them stopped them from coming up to him.

Later on, he realized that even though they didn't come out and make fun of him to his face, they still talked to each other. He'd left his old town, thinking a new start would change all of that, but whenever he went through here, he could hear their hushed conversations if he paid attention to them.

"Can you see his face?"

"Not well, but I think there's a third eye."

"Surely, there isn't. There can't be."

"Then why did it look directly at me?"

Foolishness. A third eye, indeed! And if he had a third eye, how would it even see the person when his hat was so low over his forehead? Didn't people think these things through before they said them?

He forced his attention to the clumping sounds the horses made as their hooves pounded the dirt road. By the time he made it to the jailhouse, he couldn't help but notice that a group of people had gathered nearby to watch him.

Travis turned his back to them, got down from the wagon, and stumped to the jailhouse. People like Allie had no idea how lucky there were. They could walk through town without people thinking they had some deformity like a third eye.

Don't dwell on it, Travis. There are some things you can't change, and your face is one of them.

He stepped into the jailhouse, glad to shut the door—and the onlookers—behind him.

Eric glanced up from the potbelly stove where he was pouring a cup of coffee. "Hi, Travis. Is something wrong with Allie?"

"No, she's fine. I came here to talk about Carl." He glanced at the cells and saw that Ida Conner was sitting on a bed, her arms crossed and a frown on her face. He wished he'd taken the time to give the full place a careful inspection before talking. Pulling his hat further down over his forehead so she wouldn't see his face, he added, "It should be done in private."

Eric nodded then went over to Ida. "Here's some coffee," he told her.

"I don't want the coffee," she snapped. "I want out of here."

"You should have thought about that before you started badmouthing your brother-in-law."

"I wasn't badmouthing him. I caught him hiding a woman's dress under the seat of his wagon, and I know that dress didn't belong to his wife. There's something suspicious going on with him."

"He already explained that. The dress was a gift for his wife."

She snorted. "Violet wouldn't wear a dress with that many buttons. She likes the ones you pull over your head because they're easier to put on. But since you're a man, you don't even know how important that is."

"Well, since Jerry's also a man, it stands to reason that he didn't think of it, either. Implying that he's having an affair is terrible, Ida. Just plain terrible. He's the superintendent of the school for goodness sake."

She stomped her foot on the floor and glared at him. "He is having an affair! The only reason he got rid of that dress was to hide the evidence."

"Oh come on," Eric replied. "If he was having an affair, the woman in the dress would have taken it back home with her. She wouldn't have run off naked while he held onto it."

"He is having an affair!"

"Stop it. I won't tolerate any more of these rumors. While you're in here, I want you to think about the damage you're doing. If for no other reason, you need to think of his children and the effect this will have on them."

"Jerry should have thought of his children before seeking another woman's bed."

Eric looked as if he was ready to yell at her, but then he glanced over at Travis and shut his mouth. Shooting her a scowl, he left her and went over to Travis.

It was on the tip of Travis' tongue to apologize for standing right there and listening to their conversation but Eric said, "Let's go in the other room."

With a nod, Travis followed him to the little room where they would be safely away from Ida's hearing. The last thing

Travis needed was for Ida to tell everyone about what happened with Carl.

"You said you have something to tell me about Carl?" Eric asked in a low voice.

"I just came from his place. Someone attacked him."

Eric stiffened. "Is he alright?"

"He's fine."

"Did you see who did it?"

"No. By the time I got to his place, he was lying in the stream. He was unconscious, and he was on his back. He said a man came up behind him and shoved his face into the water. The man threatened to kill him if he didn't confess to killing Lydia."

"Does he have any idea who this man was?"

Travis shook his head. "The man whispered, and Carl didn't get a look at his face. The man also knocked him on the back of his head before he left."

"What about you? Did you see anyone or anything unusual?"

"No, I didn't," Travis replied. "All I know is that Carl's not safe, and he's too afraid to tell you in case the killer goes after him again."

"As long as the killer didn't see you go to Carl's property, then he shouldn't know you told me about this." Eric rubbed his jaw. "Are you sure the person who threatened Carl was a man?"

"Carl says the person had him pinned in the stream. Granted, Carl's not the strongest man in town, but he can hold his own against a woman."

"Yes, you're right. A woman would only have an advantage if she had a weapon, and it sounds like there weren't any weapons involved."

"No, there weren't. The person used his physical strength against him."

"Well, at least we can cross off Hank from the list of suspects."

"You thought Hank might have killed Lydia?" Travis asked.

"He's one of the suspects on my list. It turns out Lydia was expecting a child. Hank has money tucked away, and Lydia could have used the news of a child to blackmail him. You know how Hank is when it comes to money. I thought he might have been desperate enough to do something to stop her."

"How do you know she was with child?"

"I wasn't satisfied with the original report the doctor gave me. He only did a brief examination, and it didn't give me any clues I could use. So I had her body dug up and sent it back to him last week. I stayed with him while he cut her open. I was grasping at straws, but the gamble worked. The doctor figures she was probably five months along."

"You think the father is the killer?"

Eric nodded. "I think she told the father of the child, and I think he panicked and killed her to keep her quiet."

"Well, she was married to Carl. Is there any chance he was the father?"

"I know he was trying to get her in the family way because of the gold he thinks is in the stream on his land, but she was too far along in the pregnancy for him to be a serious consideration. The two hated each other. There's no way he would have taken her to his bed unless he absolutely had to, and he didn't know about his father's will when she conceived."

Travis hadn't realized Carl and Lydia had such a bad marriage. The few times he'd talked to Carl, Carl hadn't mentioned her, and Travis had never talked to Lydia. Until he saw her corpse, he hadn't even known what she'd looked like. What a terrible thing to be married and miserable. Travis could say one thing about his unexpected marriage. He thought Allie had a sweet disposition about her. She was certainly thoughtful to make him meals even though she didn't have to.

"Hank might be sixty-two, but he's still able to get a woman in the family way," Eric said, interrupting his thoughts. "The problem is that he's too thin to be able to hold a young man like Carl in the stream. We need someone who's strong enough to do that. Off the top of my head, I can think of several men who fit that description. The good news is, it helps narrow things down."

In that case, it was a good thing Travis came by. "I'll go out and check on Carl from time to time. If I see anything suspicious, I'll let you know."

"Thank you, Travis. I want to make sure I don't convict the wrong person."

"I had no idea it could be so difficult to find a murderer."

"Whoever did it was careful to cover his tracks, but, like with anything else, something will come to light sooner or later. The fact that he went after Carl tells me this news about Lydia's pregnancy has him scared. And when men are scared, they're likely to let a clue slip. I don't think it'll be long now before we find him."

Travis hoped Eric was right because he'd sure hate it if someone was after him to confess to a murder he didn't commit. Deciding he'd be vigilant to keep an eye on Carl's property, he left the jailhouse.

Chapter Nine

A week later, Travis caught someone coming up to Carl's property. It was just past noon, and Travis was riding through the land. Travis figured Carl was hiding in the cabin since he didn't see him anywhere.

Travis slipped off his horse and tied it to a tree. He crouched around one of the trees and watched as the person continued walking. After a minute, he realized the person was a woman, and more than that, she didn't seem to be going toward Carl's cabin or the stream. Her steps were too random. She didn't seem to even know where she was going.

Realizing she didn't pose a threat to Carl, he stopped hiding and headed in her direction. He tipped his hat low over his forehead then called out, "Ma'am, do you know where you are?"

She paused and glanced his way. From the distance, he couldn't make out who she was, but she must have recognized him, for she screamed and ran off in the opposite direction.

He chased after her. "I'm not going to hurt you," he called out to her. "I think you're lost. I can help you get back to town."

Apparently, his words weren't reassuring since she continued running. She was no match for him, of course. He might be big, but he could outrun a woman. He caught up to her just as she tripped over a tree root and fell on her face.

"Here, let me help you," he said, reaching for her.

"Stop! Don't touch me!" She turned over, and it was then he saw it was Ida Conner. When their eyes met, she let out a piercing scream.

He jerked back. What on earth was she doing that for? He hadn't even touched her.

"You get away from me, you monster," she said, her voice trembling as she struggled to her feet. "Don't you dare touch me! I'll have my husband hunt you down and shoot you if you do."

She tried to run again, but she let out a startled cry and fell back to the ground, this time landing flat on her behind. She got up again and limped away from him. This was pointless. Even if he'd wanted to hurt her, she couldn't escape, especially when it was apparent she'd sustained an injury the first time she fell.

"Ida, I'm not going to hurt you," he said as he followed her, careful not to get too close lest she try to run again and suffered more injuries because of it. "I just want to help you get back home."

"Who says I want to go home?" she snapped, glancing over her shoulder.

His eyebrows furrowed. He didn't sense she was angry with him, but she was definitely angry at someone. "If you don't want to go home, then where do you want to go?"

"I don't know."

"You don't know?"

"I just needed time to myself." Still limping away from him, she added, "That sheriff treated me like a child, and my husband let him do it."

"Are you running from town because Eric put you in the jailhouse?"

"No. I'm taking a much needed break because my idiot husband thinks that just because I'm a woman, I don't have enough sense to know when his brother's having an affair." She stopped then and turned to face him. "I gave twenty years of my life to that ungrateful man, cooking and cleaning up after him, and I've been raising his children, too." She pointed her finger at him. "That's no easy feat, you know. All you men do is talk about how hard you work, but I'm telling you, no one works harder than a woman."

He didn't know enough about Ida or her husband to consider her argument, so he opted to take her word for it. It was apparent she was frustrated. She probably had a right to be. Even so, wandering around in an unfamiliar place wasn't a smart idea. Who knew if she'd end up seriously hurt, or worse?

"When are you going to return home?" he asked.

"Why do you want to know?"

"Because it's not safe for a woman to be out here by herself. There are large animals out here that will attack you."

Her eyes widened as if she'd just remembered something, and she turned to hurry away from him as fast as her limp would take her.

He sighed. "I'm not an animal. I'm a human being." Why was he wasting his time? She had her mind made up. "Look, I won't touch you, alright? But this isn't a safe place to be, especially when it gets dark." When she didn't reply, he added, "Think of what's best for your children. You want to be safe for their sake, don't you?"

Her steps slowed then, an indication he'd finally gotten through to her.

Encouraged, he said, "If you don't want to go home tonight, then at least stay at my place. My wife can take care of you until you're ready to go home. You won't have to deal with me once we're there, either. You and my wife will have the entire cottage to yourself."

She stopped and turned back to him. "Where do you live if you don't live with your wife?"

It was on the tip of his tongue to tell her he lived in a cave since she seemed to think he was a monster. Monsters, after all, didn't live in civilized places like houses or buildings.

A sound from behind him caught his attention, so he glanced over his shoulder in time to see Carl hurrying their way, a rifle in his hand.

"It's alright," he called out to Carl. "It's just Ida Conner."

Carl slowed down but asked, "Is anyone hurt?"

"No." Then, remembering her limp, Travis added, "Well, she fell and hurt her leg."

"It's my ankle," she said.

"Her ankle hurts," he amended.

Carl waited until he reached them before he asked her, "Is it broken?"

"I don't know," she replied. "I've never had a broken ankle to know what it feels like."

"We should take a look at it," Travis said, taking a step toward her.

"Oh no, you don't!" She held out her hand to stop him. "I won't have any man but my husband or the doctor taking a look at my ankle. Some things are too private, and my ankle is one of them."

"Will you let my wife take a look at it?" Travis asked.

She paused. "Well, I suppose there's nothing wrong with another woman looking at it. But will she recognize a broken ankle if she sees one?"

Travis shrugged. "I don't know. If she doesn't, she can take you to the doctor."

She glanced from him to Carl.

"I can tell if an ankle's broken," Carl told her.

"Maybe you can, but I won't have my reputation soiled by showing my ankle to either one of you. Gossip gets spread much too fast in this town," she replied.

"We know," both Travis and Carl said at the same time.

Surprised, Travis looked over at Carl, wondering what he had to deal with from the people in town. Up to now, he'd assumed he was the only one who had to deal with the whispers and snickers. But maybe he wasn't.

Ida's face went red from embarrassment, and she lowered her gaze.

"Do you trust us enough to carry you to Carl's wagon so we can take you to my place?" Travis asked. "Like I said, my wife can tend to your ankle."

She glanced back up at them, her eyes going from one to the other. "You won't take liberties with me?"

Carl snorted. "After being married to Lydia, the last thing I want to do is touch another woman."

Her eyebrows furrowed, and God only knew what she was thinking. Travis said, "We promise to be respectful the entire time." When she didn't seem convinced, he held his hand out to Carl. "Let's give her the rifle. I think it'll make her feel safe."

After a moment, Carl handed it to him, and he held it out to her. "There. You hold onto this while I carry you. If Carl or I do anything wrong, you can shoot us."

She stared at the rifle and gulped. "I've never touched a gun before."

"There's nothing to it," he said. "This is the trigger. You pull it and the bullet will fly right out." When she didn't grab the rifle, he added, "You can shoot over there to test it out if you want. Just make sure to tuck this part," he gestured to the end of the gun, "to your shoulder."

She shifted from one foot to another and let out a yelp. She knelt down to rub her ankle.

"You're in no shape to walk all the way to his wagon," Travis said.

She let out a sigh. "You're right. I'm not." She took a deep breath then accepted the rifle with a trembling hand.

For a moment, Travis questioned the wisdom in handing the rifle to someone who was obviously frightened. She could very well pull the trigger without meaning to. From the way Carl frowned, he could tell the other man had the same apprehension he did. But it was what it was.

"I'll be careful not to touch you anywhere inappropriate," Travis assured her. "Are you ready to be picked up?"

Clutching the rifle to her chest, she nodded.

Well, at least her hand wasn't on the trigger. That made him feel much better about this arrangement. He bent down and scooped her up into his arms.

To his surprise, she let out a chuckle.

He looked at her, and too late did he realize that, by carrying her, he was giving her the perfect view of his scarred face. Was she laughing at him like so many others had in the past?

She cleared her throat then explained, "It was fun being swept up like that. My husband only picked me up once, and that was on our wedding day."

Relaxing, he returned her smile. "Well, you hardly weigh anything. It won't be any trouble taking you to the wagon." He turned to Carl. "I'll follow you."

Carl glanced at the rifle, which Ida was still holding, though not as tightly as before. With an uneasy look, he turned his back to them and led the way to his barn.

***

Allie was pulling weeds out of the long-ago abandoned flowerbed by the cottage when she saw the familiar frame of her aloof husband guiding a wagon up the hill leading to their home. Squinting, she noticed that a woman was sitting next to him, and a man was riding a horse behind them.

She had to pinch herself to make sure she wasn't dreaming. Not only was Travis coming her way in broad daylight, but he was with other people.

Putting aside her gardening tools, she walked to the clearing between the cottage and building and waited for them. As they neared, she realized the man on the horse was Carl Richie. She didn't recognize the woman sitting in the wagon, but the woman was grimacing and rubbing her ankle.

She couldn't help but try to get a better look at Travis' face. As he pulled to a stop, she darted over to his side of the wagon. The ploy worked. For the first time, she got a good look at his face. He didn't have an extra eye, nor did he have two noses or some other deformity. He looked just like any other person. Except he had scars on his face.

She blinked in surprise. Why did he insist on hiding his face? There was nothing scary about him at all.

He ducked his head, so he was no longer in her viewing range. "Ida Conner has a sore ankle," he said as he set the brake. "Would you mind taking a look at it?"

Ida Conner? As in *the* Ida Conner who'd spread rumors about Caroline? Forcing aside her shock, Allie said, "My uncle was a doctor, and I helped him on occasion. I'll see what I can do for her."

Carl gave Allie a wave before he led Travis' horse into the barn. Meanwhile, Travis helped Ida down from the wagon and then carried her to the cottage.

Curious, Allie followed him. This was the most time she'd spent in Travis' company, and never in a million years did she think Ida Conner's being hurt would be the reason for it.

Travis gently placed Ida in the chair. He made a move to leave the cottage, but Allie blocked his exit. If she didn't speak to him right now, who knew if she'd ever have the chance again?

"Do you have anything I can use to help her?" Allie asked. "She might need bandages."

She could tell by the way he winced that he hadn't expected her to need anything from him. But after a moment, he said, "I have bandages in the building."

"Good. Wait here. I'll tell you what we need once I look at her ankle," she replied and made her way over to Ida.

"I can't expose my ankle in front of him," Ida whispered. "He's not my husband, nor is he a doctor."

"Oh, well…" She glanced over at Travis. If she let him leave right now, she'd lose the opportunity to get more acquainted with him. "Travis, would you mind turning around while I check her ankle?" Before Travis could argue it might be better if he just left, she added, "It'll only take a minute."

Sighing in resignation, he turned his back to them and waited.

Relieved, Allie looked at Ida. "Which ankle is it?"

With a cautious glance at Travis, Ida lifted the hem of her dress and showed her. Allie unbuttoned her boot, a process which took longer than she expected, and carefully removed it so she didn't make things worse for the woman. She then lowered the woman's stocking. Ida's ankle was swollen and showing early signs of bruising.

Right away, Allie could see what the problem was. "The ankle's broken."

Ida gasped. "Broken?"

"It's not serious, but it'll take about a month to a month and a half to heal. If Travis has the things I need, then I can take care of it. Then you won't have to go to the doctor."

Allie went over to Travis. He made a move to tilt his head away from her, but she reached up and took his hand and squeezed it. Her maneuver made his eyes widen as he glanced her way.

"You have nothing to hide," she whispered.

His eyebrows furrowed.

She smiled, and in a louder voice, she said, "You said you have bandages. Do you have something I can use as a splint so she won't be able to move her ankle? Also, do you have something she can use to help her walk? She'll need to stay off her ankle as much as possible for a while."

"Yes, I can make those things."

Make them? Oh, of course! She recalled the stacks of used items in the building. He had the materials on hand to make what she needed.

"Do you know how long it'll take to get them ready?" she asked.

"I have bandages already, so I can get those to you now. But the splint will take about fifteen minutes to make. The crutch will take longer. Probably an hour or two."

"Bring the bandages when the splint's ready." Since he didn't leave right away, she added, "Is there something you want to tell me?"

He shook his head. "I just want to make sure there's nothing else you need."

"Not at the moment." As he left the cottage, she thanked him then returned to Ida.

Chapter Ten

Travis' heart was beating much too fast as he left the cottage. Allie had looked directly at him. She'd been curious about him. That much he knew. What he hadn't expected was her response to his scars. Her gaze had gone to them, but it hadn't stayed there. Sure, she'd said he had nothing to hide, but that did little to reassure him of anything. One of the girls from his hometown had told him that, too, before she brought him to meet her friends and asked him to take off his hat. Then she and all her friends had laughed at him.

He didn't think Allie was like that girl, but it still brought up enough of the memory, which made him uncomfortable. So it was with great relief that he headed for the barn to check on Carl. Carl, at least, was safe.

Travis entered the barn just as Carl was putting the saddle away. "I could go back with you," he told Carl. "In case the killer tries to threaten you again."

"No," Carl replied. "I'm a grown man. Not a child. I need to deal with this myself. Besides, I got my rifle."

"Yes, but since you'll be in a wagon, you can't move out of the killer's way quickly if he tries to shoot you."

"If he shoots, he shoots. Maybe it'll put me out of my misery."

"You don't mean that," Travis called out as Carl was on his way out of the barn.

Carl stopped and turned to him. "How do you know I don't mean it? You think the worst thing that can happen to a man is that he gets scars on his face? Do you think you're the only one who has to deal with the gossip in town? There are lots of things that can happen to make a man wonder if everything in his life is a huge waste of time."

"I know things aren't pleasant for you in this town." Especially not with the threat looming over his head. "But you can get out of here if you find the gold you're looking for. Unlike me, you can start fresh in a new town. Your face is like any other man's. My scars do matter. It's why people say I'm a monster, and that doesn't change no matter where I go."

Travis took a deep breath. He hadn't intended to blurt that out. Looking away from Carl, he excused himself and passed him so he could go to the building. He still had to make that splint and crutch for Ida. Standing around and trying to convince Carl he still had it better than him—even with the other things going on—was pointless. Unless someone had to deal with the scars themselves, they'd never truly understand what he had to go through.

"If having scars is the worst thing you have to worry about, you're lucky," Carl called out as he followed him.

Travis' steps slowed so Carl could catch up to him.

And before Travis could speak, Carl continued, "I'd take scars any day over a worthless father who thought more of his illegitimate family than his real one. I'd also take them over the miserable woman he made me marry. I saw the way Allie looked at you when she saw your face, and she showed you far more concern than I ever received from Lydia. If that's the kind of thing scars will get me, then I'll gladly trade you."

Carl stared at him, as if he expected Travis to reply, but Travis didn't know what to say. Travis' father had been a good man, a decent man. Even to his dying day, he still loved Travis' mother, and Travis never doubted his father's love for him. Had it not been for his father, he didn't know if he would have had the strength to keep going when everyone in town ridiculed him.

As for Allie… Could it be true? Did she really mean it when she told him he had nothing to worry about? His looks hadn't disgusted her?

"Forget it," Carl muttered. "Like Abe, you don't realize how good you have it."

Travis thought to go after him while he climbed into the wagon. But what good would it do? Carl was upset, and after what he'd told Travis, Travis couldn't blame him. Carl had scars, too. His scars just happened to be the kind people couldn't see.

Recalling the things Ida needed, Travis went to the building. He found an old piece of wood and whittled it down until it made a suitable splint for a woman's ankle. Once he was done, he grabbed some bandages from the few medicinal supplies he had then carried the objects to the cottage.

When he got there, he took a moment to look into the window. Allie was handing Ida a cup of coffee, and if he was right, she was making a pot of stew on the cookstove. His mouth watered. Allie had made stew last week, and it was one of the best meals he'd ever had. He wasn't sure what seasonings she used to make it taste so good, but he couldn't wait to have more of it.

His gaze went back to Allie who had bent down to check on Ida's ankle. Right. The bandages and splint. He went to the door and knocked on it.

When Allie opened it, he had to resist the urge to lower his face so she wouldn't see his scars. "I think the splint is the right size and shape for someone as small as Ida."

"Thank you, Travis."

She took the items from him, and he had to force himself to keep still when their fingers brushed because the contact made his skin tingle. He hadn't experienced any such thing when he picked Ida up. The only other time he'd experienced this was when that girl had led him over to her friends. She'd taken his hand, and like a fool, he'd thought it meant she was being nice to him.

He shoved the memory aside and focused on Allie. "I'll work on the crutch." Then, before she could reply, he hurried back to the building.

***

"Thank you for helping me," Ida told her as Allie wrapped the bandages around the splint that was holding Ida's ankle in place.

"You're welcome." Allie smiled. "I'm glad Travis had the things we needed in his building. He has so many things out there it's hard to make sense of them, but he seems to have everything."

"I've been afraid of your husband ever since he came here years ago. He always seemed more like a mystery than an actual person since people rarely ever see him. Until today, I never even saw his face." She let out an uneasy chuckle. "You probably think that's silly because he really isn't scary after all."

"I don't think it's silly. I was scared when I first came here." After a moment, Allie added, "I never came across anyone so terribly shy before."

"Do you think he's more scared of us than we are of him?"

"After seeing his face, I do. There was a boy back in my hometown of Tennessee who was attacked by a dog. The dog bit his ear off. I remember the boy was afraid people were going to make fun of him because of it, but the people were very supportive. Maybe Travis is afraid people will make fun of him because of the scars on his face."

"I never thought of it that way," Ida thoughtfully stated. "If that's the case, then it's no wonder he hides from everyone the way he does." She put her hand over her heart. "And people like me haven't been any help, either."

"It's easy to give into the rumors. The judge told me all sorts of stories about him that weren't true, and I fell for them. I spent the entire wedding night terrified he'd hurt me."

"This isn't going to be easy to admit, but I was one of the people spreading the lies about him." She bit her lower lip. "I think I see what the sheriff's been trying to teach me. Rumors really can be harmful."

Allie briefly recalled Caroline telling her that Eric had put Ida in jail for one night after Ida spread falsehoods about Caroline. At the time, Allie couldn't believe a sheriff would do that to someone because of something like gossip, but this was a small town, and things could happen in small towns that weren't accepted in larger ones.

Now, as she studied the expression on Ida's face, she suspected Ida was beginning to sincerely regret the rumors she'd spread through town. Maybe Travis' act of kindness had done far more good than anything Eric could have done.

"You know," Allie began as she rose to her feet, "it's not what we've done that matters as much as what we're going to do. You can't do anything about the past. You can only do something about the future."

Allie went over to the stew and stirred it, daring a glance outside the window, something that had become a habit ever since she came out here. Travis was still in the building. She wondered if he'd come in for supper this evening. Probably not. The idea was a silly one.

With a sigh, she set the ladle down and returned to her guest. "Would you like more coffee?"

"No, thank you. What you've given me is enough."

Allie decided to pour herself another cup. Maybe she should have invited Travis in to drink a cup with them. Sure, she'd asked him to make something to help Ida walk, and there was no doubt he was busy working on it. But she didn't have to make him think he needed to do it right away. There was certainly time to spare for some coffee.

Well, she could bring a cup out to him. Inspired, she poured him a cup. "I'm going to take this out to my husband," she told Ida. "I'll only be gone for a few minutes. Is there anything you need before I go?"

Ida bit her lower lip. "It's not my intention to impose on your hospitality, but I was wondering if I might stay here for the night? I'm so upset with my husband right now. If I see him, I'm likely to whack him on the head with a rolling pin."

Allie couldn't help but chuckle at the image of Ida doing just that. Except Ida wouldn't have to resort to using a rolling pin. She could use the crutch Travis was making her.

"You're more than welcome to stay tonight," Allie said. "I'll ask Travis to tell your husband that you're fine."

"Why?"

"Because your husband must be worried about you."

"Let him worry. It'd do him some good to remember that I'm important to him," Ida said. "He's taken me for granted for years. If he thinks something horrible happened to me, maybe he'll appreciate me again."

Noting the pain in the woman's expression, Allie relented. "Alright. I won't ask Travis to talk to your husband tonight." Maybe tomorrow, Ida would be more inclined to let her husband know she was fine. "Do you mind if I take this to Travis?" She gestured to the cup in her hand.

"Oh, I don't mind at all."

Anxious to have an excuse to talk to Travis, Allie told her she'd be back soon and left the cottage.

***

Travis caught sight of Allie heading toward the building and stiffened. Why was she coming for the crutch so soon? He'd told her it might take an hour or two to make. He glanced at the lumber on the worktable. It wasn't anywhere near to being done.

The knocking at the door made him jump. It shouldn't have. He knew she was coming. And yet, he had no idea what he should do next.

"Travis?" she called from the other side. "I brought you something to drink."

He hesitated. Did he really want to let her in? He released his breath. Yes, he did. But was it a wise move to open himself up to someone who had the potential to hurt him?

How do you know she'd hurt you?

Because everyone else has done it.

Your father didn't.

He was different. He was my father. I was a part of him.

Aren't you a part of Allie? Your father taught you that when a man married, he became one with his wife.

The doorknob turned, and Allie poked her head inside. When her gaze rested on him, she said, "I wanted to bring you a cup of coffee." Then, as if she needed to prove her point, she lifted the cup and showed it to him. "I thought you might be thirsty."

He cleared his throat then gestured to the small table by the door. "Alright."

But she didn't put it on the table and leave, as he'd hoped she would. Instead, she came into the building and closed the door behind her, an indication she meant to stay. She hadn't done this before. In fact, she hadn't even opened the door until now. And he didn't know whether to panic or be relieved. It was difficult to balance the need for safety with the need to rid himself of the aching loneliness that had been hovering over his life ever since his father died.

When she reached him, she held the cup out to him, her lips curling up into a smile. She sure was pretty when she smiled. Well, she was pretty, regardless, but it seemed to him that she was especially so when she smiled.

"You have nothing to be afraid of," she said. "I made sure not to put in too much water this time. The coffee actually tastes good."

Recalling the cup she'd left him that morning, he felt the corner of his mouth twitch upward. Honestly, he hadn't minded it. Watered down coffee was the least of his worries.

Since he didn't take the cup, she set it on the worktable next to the crutch he was making. She scanned the room. "I think it's marvelous how you can create such beautiful things from all of this." She motioned to everything in the room. "And not only are they beautiful, but they're good quality, too. Why, those kitchen chairs are the most comfortable I've ever been on. You have a wonderful gift."

Again, he didn't know how to respond. Maybe if he'd had more social interactions with people, this wouldn't be so awkward. But for that to be the case, he would have had to look like everyone else.

She turned her attention back to the crutch he was crafting. "Will you show me how you're going to make this?"

Show her? Was she serious? He hardly believed it was something that would interest a woman.

Maybe she's trying to be nice. Maybe she wants to get to know you. Maybe she really meant it when she said you have nothing to worry about, that she can accept you despite your appearance.

When she looked expectantly at him, he swallowed the lump in his throat and picked up the knife he'd been using to shape the crutch. His hand was shaking. This wasn't good. He did his best work when he wasn't nervous.

But she was patiently waiting, her hands folded in front of her and that same beautiful smile on her face. He didn't think she'd leave until he did as she wished. Well…maybe she'd grow bored of watching him and go back to the cottage.

He took a deep breath. He could do this. If he pretended he was alone, he might be able to calm his nerves enough so he'd stop trembling. Gripping the knife, he brought it to the wood and carved into it. The shavings fell to the worktable effortlessly. How he wished talking to people could be as easy as crafting a piece of wood into the shape he wanted.

"What do you do with those?" she asked.

He had to look at her so he could figure out what she was talking about. She was pointing to the wood shavings.

"I burn them," he finally replied, wincing when he caught the way his voice shook. Yes, there was no doubt about it. He had a much easier time working with things than communicating with people.

"How often do you burn things?" she asked.

He shrugged. "I think I do it a few times a year."

"I think it's an efficient way of handling your garbage. Most of the people I've talked to bury their trash. I think that's what they do in this town. Am I right?"

He nodded.

"Do you ever get the things you can use before they bury them?"

Why was she asking him all these questions? Was it because he hadn't drunk the coffee yet? Was she waiting for him to empty the cup so she could take it back to the house?

To test his theory, he picked up the cup and drank the entire thing.

"Oh, you poor thing," Allie said in alarm. "I had no idea you were so thirsty. I'll get you another cup and be right back."

Before he could answer, she took the empty cup from him, her fingers once again brushing against his and producing that same pleasurable spark he'd experienced before. He was so speechless that he couldn't stop her from hurrying out of the building.

He almost went to the door and blocked it with something heavy. Almost. But he didn't.

She'd been concerned about him. He couldn't recall a time when anyone besides his father showed a genuine concern for him. Allie wasn't pretending to be interested in him, either. She really was.

The realization should have calmed his nerves. Logically, that was the way things would play out, but knowing she wanted to get to know him only made him much more nervous. If she ignored him or had fun at his expense, it would be something he was familiar with. He'd know how to react to those things. But this concern she had was much too different. And all it did was make him panic.

She returned with a larger cup of coffee and a glass of water. "I thought I'd bring more this time," she explained. "The other cup was such a small one. I also got water in case you'd rather drink it. I like to alternate between the two myself. I know coffee can help you stay awake, but I find water to be more refreshing." She placed both on the table.

"Thank…" His voice squeaked. He cleared his throat. "Thank you."

Her face lit up. "You're welcome." He thought she might stay and watch as he continued to work on the crutch, like she had planned to before, but she added, "Ida has a headache, so I need to see to her comfort. I'll come back here when the stew is done."

He should have been relieved as she left the building, shutting the door softly behind her. He really should have been relieved, and yet, he wasn't. He was disappointed. And worse, he didn't know what to do about it.

Chapter Eleven

Allie pressed a cool cloth on Ida's forehead. Ida was lying on the couch in the parlor, her injured ankle propped up on a small pillow.

"Do you feel better?" Allie asked.

"Yes," Ida replied. "Thank you."

"Think nothing of it. It's probably for the best you stay here for the night. You need to rest."

"It seems that ever since my oldest was born, I haven't had a chance to rest at all. I have ten children."

"Ten?"

Allie couldn't imagine having that many. There was barely room in this cottage for two or three.

"All my husband has to do is look at me, and I'm expecting another one," Ida said.

"You need to tell him to stop looking your way," she teased.

She chuckled. "I keep telling him that, but he says I'm so pretty he can't help it."

"Well, you are an attractive woman."

"I used to be more so when I was younger, but it is nice he still finds me pleasing to look at even after all the years we've been married."

"It is."

Ida let out a long sigh. "Maybe I've been too hard on him. He works long hours to provide for us. If the worst he does is let me sit in a jail cell, then I have it better than other women." Her gaze met Allie's. "Don't you think it's awful when a husband is unfaithful to his wife? I mean, she gives him the best of her years, has his children, and cooks and cleans for him. Then how does he thank her? He seeks out another's bed. It just doesn't seem right to me."

"To be fair, I don't think it's right if a wife does that to her husband."

"Oh, I agree. I'm alarmed at how much of this is happening in this town. Carl's wife—the one that recently died—was with a few men around here." She patted Allie's hand. "You have nothing to worry about. Travis wasn't one of them. My Mike wasn't one of them, either."

"Is that why Carl's wife was murdered?" Allie asked.

"I think so. A lot of people think so, too. She was unfaithful to him from the moment they married. It was no secret the two never loved each other. They only married because his father arranged the match. As far as I can recall, though, Carl was faithful to her." Ida groaned. "Am I gossiping by telling you this?"

"To be honest, I'm not sure."

"Until recently, I haven't taken the time to think over what separates gossip from things people ought to know. Facts are facts. They don't change, no matter how much someone wants them to."

"Well, yes, that's true," Allie slowly replied, not sure where Ida was going with this.

Ida sat up, the cloth falling from her forehead. She grabbed it then turned toward Allie. "I think there are some things we need to tell others. Take the murder. If I knew who killed Carl's wife, then I would have an obligation to say who it was. Otherwise, I'd be just as guilty of the crime as the killer."

Allie nodded. It was hard to argue Ida's point.

"If that's the right thing to do, then why is it wrong to tell a wife that her husband is having an affair?" Ida asked. "What makes killing someone different from adultery? Both are wrong."

"I suppose you're right," Allie had to admit. Having testified in court after witnessing a murder, she had to swear to tell the truth. "There are times when we have to speak up."

"Exactly! That's what I've been trying to tell my husband. I know Jerry's his brother, but I can't keep quiet just because of that." After a moment, she added, "I know it was wrong to spread rumors about Caroline Johnson and your husband. I've learned my lesson on those things. I promise I won't do that kind of thing anymore. But I do feel I have a duty to tell what I know about Jerry. I don't care if he is my brother-in-law. He's guilty, and his actions need to come to light. It was wrong for the sheriff to put me in the cell for that one, and my husband should have understood that."

"Are you absolutely certain Jerry's guilty?"

"I am. He'd been acting strange for the past six months. I couldn't figure out why until I saw him with that green dress. Then it all made sense. I don't care what he says. It wasn't a gift for his wife for her upcoming birthday. She would never want a dress like that, and he knows it."

"Did you tell his wife?"

"Of course, I did. That's how I ended up in jail. Everyone assumes I'm just trying to spread more gossip."

Allie didn't know Ida very well, but she couldn't blame the woman for being upset. Had Ida not had a reputation for gossiping, the others might have taken her seriously. But she chose not to say this. It wouldn't do any good. Ida seemed to be sincere about changing, so the last thing she needed was for someone to be critical of her.

"Well," Allie began, "maybe after a good meal and a good night's sleep, things will look better."

"Maybe." She settled back on the couch and pressed the cloth back to her forehead. "I really do appreciate all you're doing for me."

Allie gave her a smile to say she was welcome and then went to the kitchen to check on the stew.

***

Travis had just finished the crutch when there was a knock at the door. He didn't have to look out the window to know it was Allie. His heartbeat had been faster than normal ever since she'd come in here to bring him coffee. No amount of trying to slow it down had worked. He was far too anxious—and excited—by the prospect of seeing her again to relax.

And now that she was here, he found his hands were trembling again. He took a deep breath and picked up the crutch. He almost pulled the hat low over his forehead, but she'd already seen him. She knew what he looked like. There was no sense in trying to hide his face anymore.

As he reached the door, she knocked on it again and called his name. He opened it, ready to hand her the crutch. But she was holding a tray with a bowl of steaming stew on it, so he set the crutch aside and took the tray. He'd forgotten all about this particular tray. It was one of the few things he had left of his mother. He'd put it in the kitchen when he'd first moved in but hadn't ever used it.

Now, as he took the tray, he couldn't help but note the care Allie had taken in cleaning it. No doubt, it had been covered in dust, just like so many things that had been in the cottage. But he'd spent so much time out here he'd hardly noticed it. Time had passed from one day to another until the years had blurred together.

"Thank you," he told Allie. The words seemed just as awkward as they had earlier. "The crutch is over there." He nodded toward the crutch before he carried the tray to the table.

"I'm sure Ida will get good use out of it," Allie replied.

He fully expected her to leave, so he sat at the table and picked up the spoon. When he saw her close the door behind her and walk over to him, he froze.

"Ida will be staying here for the night," she said.

Was she asking for his permission, or was she telling him this? Though the sentence had been phrased as a statement, she stared at him expectantly.

He cleared his throat. "Alright."

"I was thinking it might be best if you slept in the cottage with me."

Sleep in the cottage? With her? She couldn't be serious. He was having a hard enough time maintaining eye contact with her. How was he supposed to sleep under the same roof she was?

"I was thinking about it," she continued, "and it would arouse too many questions if Ida knew you slept out here. I don't know if she'd come out and ask them, but if she did, it would be awkward."

Oh, good heavens. She was serious! "Oh, um…" He shifted in the chair. "I don't think I'll fit on the couch all that well."

"I didn't mean for you to sleep on the couch. I meant that you would sleep in our bedroom."

His gut tightened. "And you would sleep on the couch?"

"No. I would be in our bedroom, too."

"But there's no room for me to sleep on the floor."

"The bed is big enough for two people."

She didn't really intend for him to sleep in the same bed with her. There was no way she wanted them to do that.

"Ida will sleep in the other bedroom," she went on. "This way, Ida will think we have a normal marriage."

He winced. Normal marriage. Did she mean to imply that the way they were doing things now wasn't normal? He glanced over at the makeshift bed he'd been sleeping in. Well, he supposed she was right. It wasn't normal. Normal was a husband and wife sleeping in the same bed.

"Caroline Johnson warned me that Ida has a tendency to say more than she should," Allie added. "She seems sincere about not wanting to spread gossip anymore, but I don't know her well enough to trust her. I was thinking it would be safer if we slept in the same room."

He wished he could come up with something to prove Ida wouldn't tell everyone in town they slept apart, but, unfortunately, he was familiar with Ida's reputation.

If word got out that his own wife wouldn't sleep in the same room with him… Well, he didn't think that would bode well for either him or Allie.

Forcing aside his unease, he finally said, "I'll come to bed after I finish tending to the animals."

"Thank you," she replied before she took the crutch and left him alone.

He stared at the stew. He didn't know how he was supposed to eat it now.

How was he supposed to share the same bed with her? Not only was he repulsive, but he was six-and-a-half-feet tall with a large frame. Though he wasn't fat, he wasn't exactly thin. The bed might have fit the couple who used to live in the cottage just fine, but he took up most of the space whenever he slept in it. What if he rolled over and hurt her? She was such a tiny thing. He'd never forgive himself if he hurt her. And if Ida found out, who knew what they'd say in town?

Taking a deep breath, he struggled to relax. It was only for one night. Surely, he could make it through one night. Then he could return to his bed in this building, and things would go back to the way they'd been before. He thought he and Allie had worked out a suitable arrangement this way. At least, it was something he was comfortable with.

One night. I can make it through one night.

Releasing his breath, he picked up the spoon and ate the stew. When he was done, he washed up, figuring if Allie had to endure a night with him, then the least he could do was smell nice. Afterwards, he took care of the horses, hens, and milking cow.

He then checked the traps he'd set, making sure they were hidden well enough so an animal would unknowingly step in it. They were getting low on meat, and he enjoyed the steaks Allie had made for him. She'd even put some of the savory meat into the stew tonight. He didn't know what her secret was, but she was even better at cooking than Lois—and Lois was an excellent cook.

Once there was nothing else for him to do, he took the tray and carried it to the cottage, his footsteps slowing with every step he took. Why did this have to be so difficult? Why couldn't he be like everyone else? What other husband would shy away from the opportunity to be with his wife?

From the open window near the door, he could hear Allie laughing at something Ida was telling her. Well, the two were having a good time. He supposed that worked in his favor. Maybe they'd be enjoying themselves enough where they wouldn't notice him.

"I'm telling you," Ida said, "he looked just like a monster."

He paused at the door and frowned. Were they talking about him?

"So I made him wash the mud off his face at once," Ida continued. "Then I gave him a firm talking to about trying to scare his little sister."

Travis relaxed. She was talking about her children. Not him.

Allie laughed harder. "Maybe it's good I was the oldest. I'd hate to think of my brothers playing such pranks on me. That would be horrible."

"One thing I will say is that life never gets boring with children around. And the more you have, the more interesting life gets. Why, just you wait until you have a couple. One will try to outwit the other, and there will be fights over the silliest things."

Children? Ida thought he and Allie would have children? His first inclination was to laugh at the absurdity of such a thing. But then, he supposed it was a good thing Ida believed it would happen. It meant she thought enough of him to consider he had the potential to even have them. He could take that as a compliment if he wanted, and maybe, for once, he would take a comment that way.

And this only reinforced why Allie's suggestion they sleep in the same room was the right thing to do. Ida would think they had a marriage just like everyone else. Then Allie would be saved from any needless gossip.

Steadying his resolve, he opened the door and stepped into the kitchen. From where he stood, he couldn't see the two women, nor could they see him. But even so, Allie came into the kitchen just as he shut the door.

"I'll take that," she told him as she took the tray from him. "Would you like to sit in the parlor?"

He'd come here only to sleep in the bedroom. That was it. He hadn't come in to talk to Ida.

As if she could read his mind, she gave him an apologetic smile. "I'm sorry. I didn't mean to make you uncomfortable. You may go on to bed. I'll be there after I get things ready for Ida for the night."

He glanced around the doorway and saw Ida sipping from her cup. She was reclined on the couch, her injured ankle propped up.

Allie took the bowl and spoon to the sink and started washing it. With a look in his direction, she asked, "Is there anything you need?"

He shook his head. "No," he forced out. Ida was going to see him as he went to the bedroom. There was no way around it. Lowering his voice so only Allie could hear him, he asked, "What should I tell her as I walk by?"

She finished washing the dish and spoon and set them on a towel to dry. "I'll take care of that." She held her hand out to him.

He stared at it.

"It'll be fine," she assured him, giving him that smile that seemed to light up everything around her. "I'll do the talking."

He hesitated for another moment but then took her hand. Once more, he experienced the same pleasant tingling sensation from touching her. Did she feel it, too? No. Such a thing would be silly. It was all in his mind.

She led him through the parlor and paused when Ida's gaze went to them. "Travis wanted to tell you that he hopes your ankle will heal soon," Allie said for him.

"I appreciate that, Travis," Ida told him. Then, with a tentative smile, she continued, "I'm sorry for all the things I said about you. They weren't true, and it was wrong for me to do that. I hope you might find it in your heart to forgive me, but if you don't, I'll understand."

He hadn't expected this. No one had ever apologized to him before. Allie tugged on his hand to lead him to the bedroom, but he remained still so he could tell Ida, "I forgive you."

Ida seemed relieved, and he relaxed. Well, he relaxed as much as he could, considering he was holding Allie's hand and would be sharing a bed with her that night.

Allie proceeded to lead him to the bedroom, and he stopped in the doorway. He almost didn't recognize it. There was new bedding and an assortment of feminine items lined the top of the dresser. She had even put a bouquet of wildflowers in a vase and set it in the middle of her things. Then there were pretty curtains blowing in the breeze as it came into the room.

Yes, this room definitely had her touch to it. And honestly, it looked a lot better than it had when he occupied it. Well, except for one small detail. Allie had even moved the mirror from the other bedroom into this one, and it hung above the dresser. With the room being as small as it was, he couldn't help but see his reflection. Even though he tried with all his willpower to ignore it, his gaze kept going back to it. He should have smashed the thing like he'd done with the other one. All mirrors did was taunt him. But then, why shouldn't Allie be able to look at herself? She was beautiful.

Allie let go of his hand and shut the door. "Which side do you want to sleep on?"

Since he'd made it a habit of sleeping in the middle of the bed, he had to think over this one. He supposed the safest place was by the window. That way, if he happened to sweat in the middle of the night, the breeze might ward off any unpleasant odors.

"By the window," he finally said.

Yes, he'd washed up with soap, but that didn't mean he was safe from smelling bad later that night.

Even now, he was aware of the beads of sweat lining his brow. This was ridiculous. What made him think he could survive an entire night in this room with her? This was going to be a horrifying ordeal.

She went to the bed and pulled down the blanket and sheet on his side. "I need to help Ida to her bed. After that, I'll be in."

Though his heart seemed to have stopped, he nodded. Soon, very soon, they'd be in this bed together. He wanted to keep his thoughts on just sleeping. Really, he did. He willed his mind to pretend he was in the building. If he could just pretend he was out there, then he could let his mind drift off to sleep.

But no matter how much he wanted it, all he kept thinking of was that he'd be spending the night with Allie. He glanced at her, afraid she might know this, but she only gave him another smile as she slipped out of the room and shut the door behind her.

He closed his eyes and tried to calm his racing heart. If she had any idea what he was thinking, she'd be horrified. Any woman would be horrified at the thought of being with him. But just because he was thinking it, it didn't mean he was going to do it.

No. He'd keep his hands to himself. And to prove it, the only things he took off were his hat and his boots. The rest of his clothes would stay on for the entire night. Then, at least, Allie would know she was safe. Decision made, he went to bed, dreading the moment when she'd come in to join him.

Chapter Twelve

An hour passed before Allie went to the bedroom. She softly opened the door, just in case Travis was already asleep. In the moonlight streaming in through the parted curtains, she saw that his eyes were closed. She slipped into the room and closed the door, quiet as she did so.

To her surprise, he was still dressed. Maybe she should have offered to bring in his nightclothes from the building. She'd do so now if he wasn't already asleep. Sleeping in one's clothes wasn't all that comfortable, but she wasn't going to wake him so he could change. He was probably exhausted from the day's events. He had, after all, brought Ida back here and made her things to help her heal. If she'd done all that, she might have fallen asleep as soon as her head hit the pillow, too.

She'd been apprehensive about getting undressed in front of him, but since he was already asleep, she didn't hesitate to remove her clothes. Yes, she supposed it was silly to be worried about slipping into her nightshirt with her husband in the room. If theirs was a normal marriage, she might not even think twice before doing it. But they didn't have a normal marriage. And as much as she was trying to get to know him, he remained every bit a mystery to her.

Once she had her nightshirt on, she brushed her hair and then braided it to keep it from tangling through the night. The familiar routine did much to calm the butterflies in her stomach. While it was her idea for them to spend the night together in this room, that didn't mean she hadn't been anxious about what would happen.

With a glance over her shoulder, she noted his eyes were still closed. Maybe it was just as well he was sleeping. She'd wanted to talk to him again, but it was hard to have a conversation with someone who was too shy to reply to her questions.

Which brought something else to mind. What if they spent the rest of their lives this way? What if he stayed out in the building and rarely talked to her?

Up to now, she had assumed it was a temporary arrangement. But what if it wasn't? What if this was going to be permanent? Could she be happy with that? She glanced over at him again. Did she have a choice? If he didn't want to spend time with her, then what could she do about it?

Not sure how she felt about this unexpected possibility, she made her way over to the bed. He had left plenty of room on her side, something that surprised her since she had expected him to take up more room.

Shrugging, she slipped into the bed, trying to be careful so she wouldn't wake him. If he was hesitant to hold her hand, she wasn't sure what he'd do if he woke up with her right next to him in bed. Fortunately, he didn't stir from his slumber.

After a moment's debate on how she should go to sleep, she decided to roll onto her side, her back to him. That might be the safest position to choose. If he happened to wake up, he shouldn't be startled if she wasn't facing him.

She took a deep breath and released it. This arrangement was awkward. There was no denying that. But it was doable. Relaxing, she closed her eyes, and surprisingly, she soon drifted off to sleep.

***

No matter how hard Travis tried, he couldn't fall asleep. He thought if he imagined himself on the makeshift bed in the workshop, he would manage to do it, but he was very much aware of the fact that he was in his bedroom—and he wasn't alone.

The gentle rise and fall of Allie's chest notified him that she'd fallen asleep. How he envied her the ability to fall into blissful contentment so easily. But then, why should it be any other way? She was beautiful and sweet. She had no trouble attracting people.

First, Phoebe and Caroline had come out to visit her a couple of times. Then, Lois came by to talk to her, and from the way Lois had been smiling on her way to her buggy, Travis could tell they'd had a good time. And today, Allie met Ida, and the two had been laughing and enjoying each other's company. He suspected no matter who Allie came across, she never had trouble getting along with anyone.

He didn't want to envy people. He knew it only led to discontentment. *Your job is to be the best Travis Martin you can be,* his father had told him. Travis had an easier time focusing on that when he was alone. But as soon as he was near people and saw how easily they got along, that sneaky feeling of envy would slip in and remind him that he was inferior, that he would always be an outcast.

If only he could be content with things as they were.

Allie rolled onto her back, and to his horror, she turned over to face him then snuggled up against him. Should he wake her up and urge her to roll back over? He'd been fighting his erection ever since he watched her change into her nightshirt.

He shouldn't have looked. He had scolded himself for peeking through his eyelashes at her, but he'd never seen a naked woman, and his curiosity had gotten the best of him. He might never fit in with the world, but that didn't mean he wasn't still human, despite what the gossiping people in town said about him. He'd have to be truly abnormal not to want to see a woman naked, especially when she was married to him.

The memory of how she looked only made things that much more difficult when she was snuggled up to him. If he wanted to get any sleep tonight, he was going to have to wake her so she'd roll back over.

"Allie?" he whispered. When she didn't respond, he shifted so that he could tap her shoulder. "Allie?"

But instead of waking up, she let out a contented sigh and put one of her legs over one of his. He inwardly groaned. This was even worse than what she'd been doing before.

What was he supposed to do? He couldn't give into the desire to touch and kiss her the way his body was urging him to do. For one, he didn't have her permission. And two… Well, two… He'd probably be lacking in that area just as he was lacking in social graces and good looks.

After a long debate over whether or not he should roll her over, he finally decided to wrap his arm around her shoulders and let her continue sleeping. Even if it was for this one night, it would be nice to hold her. The experience was a pleasant one, after all.

Yes, he likely wouldn't sleep. Yes, it was uncomfortable to lie still when he was fully erect. But what other time would he get to do this? Ida would be returning home tomorrow, and there would be no excuse to be in this bedroom. He'd take tonight for what it was and enjoy it. For once, he could pretend he was a normal husband in a normal marriage. And for once, he wouldn't have to feel so lonely.

***

When Allie woke the next morning, she was alone in the bed. She sat up and rubbed her eyes. She'd slept better last night than she had since she arrived here. Last night, she hadn't woken up a couple of times. She'd felt safe and protected, much like she'd been when she was a little girl and would sleep with her parents when the shadows scared her.

She got out of bed and checked the pocket watch one of her brothers had given her before she left Tennessee. It was after nine. She blinked and looked at it again. How was it possible she'd slept so late? She hurried to get into her dress and brushed her hair. She should have made breakfast by now. Travis and Ida would be hungry.

After she pinned her hair back into a bun, she quickly made the bed and then left the room. An apology was on her tongue when she saw the sandwiches waiting for her and Ida on the kitchen table. Next to them was a pot of freshly brewed coffee and two cups.

Her gaze went to the building. If she guessed right, Travis was already there. She turned back to the table. Since there were only enough for her and Ida, she surmised he'd taken his sandwich and coffee out with him. She sighed in disappointment. She shouldn't have expected him to stay for breakfast. She should have known he would sneak out first thing in the morning.

As tempted as she was to check on him, she thought better of it and went to Ida's room. She knocked on the door.

"Come in," Ida called out.

She opened the door and saw that Ida was struggling to fasten the buttons on her boot. Her injured foot, however, was bare. Ida glanced over at her and smiled. "I should never have taken the ability to bend down for granted."

Returning her smile, Allie went over to her and knelt by the boot. "I'll help you. Give me the hook."

Ida handed it to her, and Allie proceeded to fasten the buttons. "I really wish I'd been sensible when I bought these boots. The buttons are downright impossible."

Allie chuckled. "They are pretty boots. I can see why you wanted them."

"I couldn't resist them when I saw them in the catalogue. I asked Mike to get them for me for my birthday. So really, they're a gift."

"I bet he was relieved he didn't have to guess what you wanted."

"He was. Usually, I don't splurge on something so expensive, but he happened to find a bit of gold and wanted to buy me something nice. The only catch was, I had to be the one to pick it out."

"That was nice of him."

"It was. That was three years ago. The boots are such good quality. They've stood the test of time."

Noting the wistful tone in Ida's voice, Allie glanced up at her.

Ida wiped a tear from her eye. "I had a lot of time to think last night. Even as mad as Mike made me, one thing I know for sure is that he'd never take another woman to bed. I feel so awful for Violet. Violet is Jerry's wife. She's a nice woman. She doesn't deserve what he's doing to her, and what's worse is that they have two children. I honestly don't know what I'd do if I was her."

Allie fastened the last button then stood up. "Are you sure Jerry's having an affair?"

Ida nodded. "This isn't like the thing I did to Caroline Johnson. I'm not assuming there's more to things than there really is." After a moment, she cleared her throat. "It might not even matter. I don't know if Violet believes me. Jerry might keep getting away with it."

Ida reached for the crutch, and Allie helped her to her feet. "How is your ankle this morning?" Allie asked.

"Still sore, but that's to be expected."

"Are you ready to go back to town, or would you like to stay here for another night?"

"I think I'm ready to go back. I can't stay mad at Mike for long. Even if he has a tendency to think everything I do around the home isn't as draining as his job, he's a good man. It's funny," she mused. "I thought I was going to teach him to appreciate me more, but it turns out, I'm the one who learned the lesson. It's a wonderful feeling to know your husband will always be faithful to you. Well, you know how that is. Travis wouldn't have an affair, either."

Surprised, Allie said, "I thought you didn't know Travis all that well."

"I don't need to know him to tell that. I saw the way he looked at you. He looks at you the same way Mike looks at me. Well," she amended, "when I'm not embarrassing him by spreading needless rumors."

Allie wasn't sure how to respond. To her, Travis was such a mystery. Yes, he'd been kind and thoughtful to her. But she had no idea what he was thinking. Was Ida seeing things as they really were, or was she seeing things as she wanted to—just like she had with Caroline?

"Travis made us sandwiches," Allie said, following Ida to the kitchen. "It's nothing fancy, but I think it was sweet he did that before he started working in the building."

"I have ten children and a limited amount of money to feed them with. Soup and sandwiches are pretty much what I live on." Ida smiled at her. "I'm not hard to please when it comes to food. As long as it's not burnt, I'll eat anything." She shrugged. "Well, sometimes I have eaten burnt things, too."

Amused, Allie hurried to pull out a chair for her and helped her into it. She put the crutch aside and poured her a cup of coffee. "I suppose with all those children, it's hard not to burn something once in a while."

"Isn't that the truth. You'd be surprised how many emergencies happen in the course of one day. And," she shot Allie a pointed look, "when I say emergency, I mean one kid had the nerve to stare at another one, or both kids want to play with the same toy at the same time."

Even as Ida spoke, Allie noted the love she had for her children. Yes, Ida wasn't perfect. Allie still couldn't blame Caroline for not liking her. But it seemed to Allie that Ida had some redeeming qualities. If she was sincere about no longer gossiping, then maybe Caroline and others might see those redeeming qualities, too.

Chapter Thirteen

"You want me to take Ida into town?" Travis blurted out.

"I don't know the way," Allie replied as she stood by the kitchen table he was in the process of sanding. "There are so many twists and turns along the way that I wouldn't even begin to know how to get back."

As much as he hated to admit it, she was right. This wasn't an easy place to get to, which was why he bought it. It was a nice buffer between him and the people in town.

"I know you don't like being in town," she continued, "but you won't be going alone. I'll be with you."

He let out a shaky breath. "The people won't make fun of you. At the most, they'll feel sorry for you because you're stuck with me."

"Oh Travis," she said as she walked around the table so she could stand by him, "I think what those people say about you is wrong. Caroline's right. You're nothing like they claim. You have some scars, but that doesn't make you ugly."

Without meaning to, he snorted.

"It's true," she insisted. "When I look at you, I don't see anything wrong with you. You don't scare me."

Scare her? People were scared of him?

"Maybe that didn't come out right," she said.

But it's what she meant so why not just come out and say it?

"Travis," she began, "I know you can't change their opinion. It's not even worth a try. But," she took his hand and squeezed it, "what they think doesn't matter. It's what we think that's important."

Despite the heat rising up his face, he forced out, "That's easy for you to say. You never had to bear the brunt of their gossip."

"You're right. I haven't. I don't know what it's like to be you. All I know is what it's like to be me. And from my experience, you've done everything you can to make me comfortable here. When I look at you, I see a man who'll do whatever he can to help others. I think you're a good person. If your wife thinks that about you, then does it really matter what the others think?"

As much as he enjoyed her touch, he pulled his hand out of hers and stepped around the table, needing to put some distance between them so he could think clearly. Something about her was having a strange effect on him, and try as he might, he couldn't put his finger on what it was.

"All we'll do is go to Ida's house," Allie said. "Afterwards, we'll come right back here."

He tapped the edge of the table, staring at the wall in front of him. Ida, if he recalled, lived on the outskirts of town, which meant he didn't have to go through it. That would mean he didn't have to expose himself to that many people.

He sighed. Ida had to get home somehow. Carl was too much of a target to do it. He had the killer stalking him. Ida's husband didn't know where she was, nor would anyone else in the town. And as Allie had pointed out, she didn't know the way. Ida wouldn't either since she hadn't been here before. Logically, there was no other option. He had to do it.

"Alright," he finally consented. "I'll take her." Glancing at Allie, he asked, "You said you'll come, too?"

She smiled, her face lighting up in a way that made him almost glad he had agreed to this. "Of course. I'll help Ida get ready."

She went halfway to the door, paused, and then came back to him. He took a step back. Yes, she was still smiling, but that didn't mean he knew what to expect.

"I don't think I've ever come across someone so skittish," she teased. "I just wanted to give you a kiss as a way of saying thank you." Then she stood on her tiptoes and kissed his cheek. "We won't be long."

He watched her as she left. Once she closed the door softly behind her, his hand went to his cheek. The kiss had been a brief one. More of a whisper than an actual kiss. But his cheek was warm where her lips had touched him. As silly as the thought was, he did entertain the notion that he might never wash his cheek again.

***

"I don't recognize any of this," Ida said as the three sat in a wagon, winding their way through the path that would take them to town. "It's no wonder I got lost. All these trees look the same."

Allie, who was sitting between Travis and Ida, took a moment to glance behind them. They had just passed a fork in the road, and if she was right, it had been the third one. She had to agree with Ida. In fact, she was surprised others didn't get lost. The place was more of a maze than a trail.

"Do you get scared out here all by yourself?" Ida asked, her gaze going between Allie and Travis.

Allie glanced at Travis, and since he didn't reply, she said, "If I was all by myself, I would get scared, but I have Travis with me. I feel safe with him."

From beside her, Travis looked as if he couldn't believe it.

Her heartbeat picking up, she wrapped her arm around his in silent assurance that she'd spoken the truth. Yes, it made her nervous to be so forward with him. It hadn't been easy to touch his hand, kiss him, or even put her arm around his, but she had the nagging suspicion the only way she was going to get him to come out of his shell was by being physically expressive with him. He seemed to respond best when she touched him.

"I can see why you feel safe with him," Ida said. "I don't think many men, or even a bear, would mess with him." With a smile, she told Travis, "I admit I was frightened yesterday when you were coming over to me. Now I realize how silly that was. You're actually a gentle person."

His eyebrows furrowed as he peeked at Ida.

"You're strong, too," Ida continued then turned her gaze to Allie. "He carried me as if I weighed no more than a feather. Mike isn't as strong. His back would have been bothering him if he'd carried me all the way from where he found me to Carl's wagon. Just how far did you think that was, Travis?"

After a moment, he shrugged. "Almost a mile, I think."

"Can you believe that? Almost an entire mile. And your back and arms aren't sore at all?"

He shook his head.

"Mike would be full of envy if he knew how strong Travis was," Ida said. "Which is why I won't mention it when I see him." She leaned forward and whispered in Allie's ear, "One thing I've learned during the course of my marriage is that husbands like to believe they're better than other men."

"That could be said for women, too," Allie whispered in return. "A wife, after all, doesn't want to take second place to another woman."

"Yes, that is true." She sat back and nodded. "I suppose both men and women are vain."

Though Travis seemed curious about their quiet discussion, he didn't ask about it. Had he been more comfortable with her and Ida, Allie suspected he might. But since that wasn't the case, he kept his thoughts to himself.

Travis led the wagon around a bend in the road, and suddenly, they had emerged out of the mass of trees and into a clearing with tall grass and a path that would take them directly into town.

Allie wasn't sure, but she thought she felt Travis breathe a sigh of relief. She could only imagine how difficult this whole process was for him. Hoping to offer him a source of encouragement, she squeezed his arm and smiled at him.

"I really do appreciate your kindness toward me," Ida told Allie and Travis. "I know I don't deserve it, but I assure you, things will be different from now on. I'll be a better person."

"I know you'll be a better person," Allie assured her since Ida seemed to need to hear someone tell her they believed her.

Who knew? With all the gossiping she'd done, maybe she was used to people not taking her seriously.

Soon, Travis pulled the wagon to a stop right in front of a modest home where a swarm of children were in disarray.

A man came running toward them, looking relieved as a couple of the younger children followed him. "Thank God," he told Ida as he held his hands up to help her down. "I thought something bad happened to you."

"So you're not mad at me for running off?" Ida asked.

"I was at first, but when you didn't come home and I couldn't find you, I feared an animal attacked you," he replied. "Or, worse, maybe the man who killed Lydia got to you, too. For all we know, there could be someone lurking around town who wants to kill more women."

"No, I'm fine. Travis and Allie Martin were kind enough to take care of me last night." She turned to Allie and held her hand out for the crutch.

Allie hurried to give it to her, just as Mike inspected her bandaged ankle.

"What happened to you?" he asked.

"I fell over a tree root," Ida said. "It was stupid. I should have been watching where I was going."

"Well, if we hadn't gotten into that fight, then you wouldn't have run off to begin with."

"You spent the night in his house?" one of the boys asked, pointing to Travis.

Allie glanced at Travis and saw him turn his face away as he lowered the hat over his forehead. Noting his embarrassment, Allie scooted back to him and wrapped her arm around his waist, hoping the small show of support might help ease his discomfort. The poor man. He had so much to offer people, but he didn't realize it.

"Yes, I did," Ida spoke up, surprising her. "Travis Martin is a good man."

"But I thought you said he was a monster," one of the girls piped up.

"I did say that, and I was wrong," Ida replied. Glancing at Allie and Travis, she added, "I'm sorry." Then she turned her attention to her children. "The sheriff was right about me. I do say things that hurt others, and that's wrong. We'd do well to heed the sheriff's advice. Only speak that which is true, and when you say something, make sure it's because you want to help someone."

"You really mean that, Ida?" Mike asked, studying her.

Ida nodded. "Yesterday taught me a lot. Travis, Allie, and Carl were kind to me even though I didn't deserve it."

"Carl?" Mike asked. "What does Carl have to do with yesterday?"

"I ended up on his property when I tripped and hurt my ankle. Travis and Carl took me to Travis', and from there, Travis and Allie made sure I was taken care of for the night."

"You're lucky Carl didn't hurt you."

"Carl wasn't going to hurt me. He was scared. He thought I was there to hurt him." When Mike didn't seem convinced, she shrugged. "It's true. I could tell it by the way he was running over to me with a gun in his hand."

"A gun?"

"He didn't use it. In fact, he let me hold it because I was scared of them at first."

"But Carl might have killed Lydia," Mike said.

"He didn't," Travis spoke up.

Surprised, everyone turned their attention to Travis, who had, up to now, done everything he could to be invisible.

Travis cleared his throat. "The person who killed Lydia threatened to hurt Carl if Carl didn't confess to the murder."

The children gasped, and Mike shooed them away. "Go on and do your chores. You don't need to be listening to this."

"But you've been saying Carl did it," a girl told him.

Mike's face went bright red. "Go on, or I'll have you milk the cow."

The girl quickly followed her brothers and sisters as they headed back to the house.

When Mike's gaze returned to Travis, he offered a hesitant smile. "I suppose Ida isn't the only one around here who says more than they should."

"I accept your apology," Ida told him and leaned on her crutch so she could kiss him.

Despite the fact that Mike still seemed embarrassed by what his daughter had blurted out, he asked, "How can you be sure the killer threatened Carl? We've heard nothing about this."

"I saw Carl lying in the stream right after he was attacked," Travis replied. "There's no way he could have inflicted those injuries upon himself. I told the sheriff about it, but we're keeping things quiet in case the killer finds out and goes after him again. Next time, he might not just leave Carl with a warning."

"Really?" Mike seemed as if he didn't know whether to believe it or not.

"He's telling the truth, Mike," Ida said. "He has nothing to gain by lying."

"Well, I suppose not."

"We need to keep this to ourselves," Ida told him. "Right now the sheriff has the advantage. As long as the killer doesn't know what we know, then Carl's safer than he'd be otherwise."

Mike considered her words. "When you put it that way, it makes sense."

"Of course, it does. We don't want someone else dying around here, do we?"

"No."

"Then there's no harm in keeping quiet unless we find out something that can help the sheriff find the killer. Allie and I were talking about it, and we decided there's a time we need to keep quiet and a time we need to speak up. This is one of those times we need to keep quiet."

"Alright."

Seeming satisfied, Ida turned back to Allie and Travis. "Thank you both very much for all your help. I'll be sure to let everyone know you're a good man, Travis."

Travis opened his mouth, as if to protest, but Allie squeezed his waist and shook her head. This was Ida's way of extending an olive branch—her way of trying to make amends for the wrong she'd done to him. And Allie saw no reason why she shouldn't do it. When Travis relented, Allie thanked Ida.

As Mike helped Ida to the house, Travis snapped the reins and led them back to the tree-lined path that'd take them home.

Chapter Fourteen

Allie assumed since Travis had spent the night with her the previous evening, he'd come into the cottage as the sun was setting for the night. But he didn't. He remained out in the building, just as he had every other night since they married.

She spent the night in a fitful sleep. Images of killers roaming around the trees kept interrupting her dreams, and she found herself bolting up in the bed, out of breath and clutching the blanket to her chest. She wouldn't have to feel this way if Travis were in bed with her.

Finally, when daylight arrived, she was able to drift off to a restful sleep. When she decided to get up for the day, she took her time getting dressed. Before last night, her nightmares here had been restricted to animals coming into the cottage to attack her because she'd left the door open by mistake. On her wedding night, she had even been wary that Travis really was a monster, like the judge had said.

But last night, she dreamt of men who were outside seeking someone to kill. It was probably because of all the talk about Lydia being murdered. If that was anything as awful as watching a man get stabbed to death on the train, she had to feel sorry for Lydia, even if she didn't know anything positive about the woman.

Thankful it was daytime, she brought in the eggs Travis had left at her door and cooked an omelet, topping it with cheese, diced tomatoes, and sliced green peppers. She glanced out the kitchen window from time to time. Would Travis come in here to eat, or would she have to bring this out to him?

What a silly question. He was planning to stay out there to eat. He'd only braved coming into this cottage when Ida had been here, and he'd wanted Ida to think they were a normal couple.

Well, Allie was done pretending, and she didn't feel like going back to how things were before. She wanted a normal marriage. Even if she didn't want to force the issue, she didn't see how she had a choice. If she didn't do something drastic, then nothing would change between them.

She placed the omelets on their plates with cut up fruit and poured two cups of coffee. After she put everything on the tray, she carried it out to the building. She paused when she reached the closed door, realizing she had nowhere to set the tray down so she could knock. A moment passed then she kicked the door with her foot.

Usually, once she knocked on the door, she headed back to the cottage. Travis would wait for a couple minutes and then open it to get the food she'd made for him. Today, she waited. She almost called out to him but thought better of it. He was skittish enough as it was. She didn't need to give him a reason to keep the door closed.

When he did open it, he gasped and shut it. The expression of shock on his face made her chuckle despite the situation.

"Travis, this tray is getting heavy," she called out.

The door opened a crack, and she saw him peeking out at her.

She shook her head. "I'm surprised. I thought after the last couple of days, you wouldn't be afraid of me anymore."

He opened the door a little more. "I'm not afraid of you."

"No?"

"No."

She didn't believe him. She didn't believe him one single bit. And it struck her as the silliest thing she'd ever come across. It was like an elephant being afraid of a little old mouse. If anyone should be afraid of another person, she should have been afraid of him!

"Travis, this whole thing is ridiculous," she said. "Are you going to hide from me forever?"

"Well…" He glanced back at the makeshift bed in the corner of the building.

"How are we ever going to have children if we only exchange little notes on each other's doorsteps?"

The words came out before she had a chance to consider them, and she could tell by the shocked expression on his face that he hadn't expected her to be so forward in her speech. She was about to apologize, but then she decided she wouldn't.

When she'd answered the mail-order bride ad, she had been excited about the prospect of having children. Just because she didn't end up with the man she thought she would, there was no reason why she should give up on the notion of ever having them. Besides, Travis would make a good father. He was kind and gentle, and considering the care he took in his work, she suspected he would be patient with them, too.

"Can I come in?" She lifted the tray. "This is getting heavy."

After a moment, he took the tray from her. She expected him to take it into the building or to the cottage, but he stood still.

"Where would you like to eat?" she asked.

"Eat? You want to eat with me?"

"That's why I brought two of everything," she replied, keeping her tone light so he wouldn't panic.

"Um…I…" His gaze shifted from the cottage to the inside of the building.

"It makes the most sense to eat in the cottage," she said. "But I'd like to eat with you, so if you're more comfortable out here, then let's eat here."

"Oh, well…"

He scanned the building, and she could only guess what he was thinking. Maybe he was searching for a reason why they shouldn't eat breakfast together. If that was the case, she might as well intervene. They needed to share meals together. Doing so would help them do other things together, and that was necessary if she ever wanted this marriage to be what it was supposed to be.

She stepped into the building, not terribly surprised when he jerked back, a little of the coffee spilling out of the cups and onto the tray. "I won't hurt you," she assured him. "I promise."

"I know you won't," he replied, though his breath slightly shook.

"Then you have nothing to worry about." She went further into the room, her gaze resting on the new kitchen table he'd been working on. "Oh, Travis!" She hurried over to the table and traced the design of a flower etched into the center of the wood. "This is truly a work of art. Back in Tennessee, there was a man who had a gift for painting. He could put anything on a canvas and make it look lifelike. You have the same gift, except you don't work on a canvas. You work on wood."

"You really like it?"

"I do." She turned to him and smiled. "I can't understand why someone who has such a splendid gift doesn't think he's worth being with."

Though his face turned pink, he said, "I don't have anything interesting to say."

"I bet you do. Anyone who has this in his mind," she gestured to the table, "has something worth saying."

He shrugged, and probably because he finally realized she wasn't going to leave him alone, he brought the tray over to the small table he usually ate at.

"When do you think the table will be ready?" she asked as she followed him.

"Um…two…maybe three days," he replied, his voice quiet.

"The kitchen will look better when that table's in there. I can't wait to see it with the new chairs. Can you?"

Again, he shrugged.

She hesitated then said, "I'd like to eat in there together once the table's in there. It'd be a shame to waste such a fine piece of furniture." She set the plates and cups in their respective spots before she put the tray aside. She pulled up a chair, sat down, and motioned to the chair across from her. "It'd be more comfortable to eat if you're sitting."

The corner of his mouth twitched up, and she relaxed, glad he showed the hint of a smile.

He sat down but didn't make a move to eat or drink anything.

Hoping it would further ease him into being with her, she picked up her fork and cut into her omelet. "One thing I don't miss about Tennessee is having to fight my brothers for food. There were four of them, and even though they were younger, they would eat so much that I had to fend them off with a ladle whenever they tried to grab something off of my plate."

He chuckled.

"Maybe I can be scary," she continued. "But I had to be if I wanted to protect my portion of the meal."

"You didn't use the ladle, did you?" he asked.

"A few times. Once was when one of my brothers was talking to me while the other was reaching for my fried chicken. So I gave them both a good whack on the head."

Still appearing skeptical, he shook his head.

"You might not believe it," she said, "but after that, they had the nicknames 'bumpy' and 'lumpy'."

Travis laughed out loud, and she found herself laughing right along with him. "And you wonder why I hide," he replied.

"You have nothing to worry about. I wouldn't hit you with a ladle."

"Then what would you do?"

Catching the gleam in his eyes, she rubbed the edge of her fork with her thumb. "You know, I'm not sure. I can't imagine you ever doing something like that. But, if you did," she glanced around the building, "I suppose if I had to do something to punish you because you took something off my plate, I would have you come in here and make me something."

"Is there anything you need?" he softly asked.

Was he making conversation with her, or was he looking for things to do? Either way, she supposed it didn't hurt to answer him. "Well, there is something I'd like. It's not something I need, but I think it would be nice to have."

"What is it?"

"Now that the inside of the cottage is done, I'm working on the flowerbed. You know, pulling the weeds so the flowers have room to grow. It'd be nice to have two chairs on the shady part of the lawn by the cottage door. I think it would be nice to sit outside when the weather's nice. One of my favorite memories of the day in Tennessee was sitting outside in the evenings. After helping my mother with my brothers, I got a chance to sit on the porch and enjoy a quiet moment outside. With the flowers in bloom, the air would smell especially sweet when a breeze passed by."

After a moment, he said, "When I moved here, the flowerbed was in good shape. The place looked a lot better back then. I didn't realize I'd let things get so bad until I started seeing everything you were doing to the place."

She took a bite of her omelet and swallowed. "The cottage, barn, and this building are in good condition. You just have overgrown weeds and vines, that's all."

"Yes, but it would look better if these things were trimmed." He paused. "I should help you get the outside in shape before I make the chair."

"Chairs. I'd like two. One for you and one for me. It'd be nice to sit outside together, don't you think?"

He glanced at the uneaten food on his plate then turned his gaze back to her. "I'm not good at talking."

"You don't have to talk. We can sit in silence, or I can do the talking for both of us. I could even tell you how I got the nickname 'hawk'."

His eyebrows furrowed. "Your nickname was 'hawk' while you were growing up?"

She nodded. "One of my brothers came up with it."

"How?"

With a playful grin, she shook her head. "Oh no, you don't. I'm not telling you until we're sitting by the flowerbed together in those chairs you'll make for us."

He seemed as if he was going to protest but said, "That's fair."

"I'm glad you agree." And hopefully, he would be so overcome with curiosity, he'd be making those chairs sooner rather than later.

He finally picked up his fork and started eating his breakfast. Offering him a smile, she continued eating hers, content to spend the rest of the meal telling him more about her brothers.

Chapter Fifteen

"Ida said you and Travis brought her home yesterday," Caroline told Allie later that day.

She and Allie were having a cup of coffee in the kitchen while Caleb was visiting Travis in the building.

"Ida was lost on Carl's land when Travis found her," Allie replied after she swallowed a sip of her drink.

"That's what she said. She also said being out here gave her a new perspective on things, and she apologized to me for spreading rumors about me shortly after I came here." Caroline put her cup down and studied Allie. "Exactly what brought about the drastic change in her?"

"To be honest, I'm not sure. I think Travis being nice to her had something to do with it, but all I really got out of our conversations was that she's been trying to figure out the difference between needless gossip and what people need to know."

"Yes, she said something about that to me, too. Apparently, the things she said about me fell into the needless gossip part. Which," she quickly amended, "is true."

"It does make for an interesting discussion, doesn't it? We all have times when we need to speak up. On my way here, I saw posters for wanted men. If I happened to see one of those outlaws, then it'd be my duty to say something."

Caroline nodded. "I hadn't thought about it that way, but it makes sense. Just like the whole thing with Lydia's murder. If someone knew something that could help my husband, then he could finally put the matter to rest. As it is, the killer is free to do whatever he wants."

"Are there any suspects?"

"Eric has it narrowed down to four people."

"Is Carl one of them?"

"No. There are a few people in town who are convinced Carl did it. I mean, it's no secret he hated Lydia, and he's not the most likable person in town. But Eric doesn't think he did it. I'm inclined to agree with him. If he thinks Carl is innocent, then I do, too."

Allie leaned back in her chair and crossed her arms. "I met Carl, and I don't think he's a bad man. I know Phoebe and Abe don't like him, but I think there's more to things than we know."

"Whatever started the rivalry between Abe and Carl, it had to do with their father. They don't share the same mother, and I'm sure that created a lot of the bad feelings between them. Then their father left Carl the stream in the will with the stipulation that he have a legitimate child by the time he turns thirty. He'll be twenty-nine in December. If he doesn't have a child, then the stream and twenty acres will go to Abe. Killing Lydia was the last thing Carl wanted to do. He can't have a legitimate child without a wife. That's why Eric believes Carl is innocent."

"That makes sense."

"Anyway," Caroline said after she took a sip of her coffee, "I didn't come out here to talk about Carl. I was wondering how things are between you and Travis."

Noting the worried expression on her face, Allie offered her friend a reassuring smile. "I'm glad I'm with him. You don't have to keep feeling guilty for marrying Eric."

"You're not just saying that to make me feel better?"

"No. I'm telling you it because it's true. Travis is a very shy person. Given how things are in town, I can't blame him. It's definitely taking a lot of work to make him feel comfortable with me, but it's worth it."

Caroline breathed an audible sigh of relief. "You have no idea how good that is to hear."

"Oh, I have a pretty good idea of how you feel. You look as if you're afraid you ruined my life whenever you ask about my marriage."

"Do I?"

"You do." With a chuckle, Allie teased, "You are absolved from guilt."

Caroline joined her in laughing. "Well, if Caleb's willing to spend time with Travis, then Travis is a good person."

"Caleb's right. He is. Travis is going to help me make the outside of the cottage look nice. I'm looking forward to seeing those pretty flowers bloom without the weeds trying to choke them out."

"You're getting Travis to come outside the workshop?"

Allie nodded, amused at the woman's surprised expression. "And when we sit outside together, I promised I would let him know why one of my brothers nicknamed me 'hawk' when we were growing up."

"Why did your brother give you such an odd nickname?"

"Well, I suppose it's safe to tell you since you won't tell him." She leaned forward. "Growing up, I could tell whenever my brothers were doing things they shouldn't. If the lid on the cookie jar wasn't secure, I knew one had eaten a cookie before mealtime. If the floor was sticky, I could tell what someone had been eating or drinking. If someone didn't like what was on their plate, I could tell who was feeding the dog under the table." She gave an amused shrug. "I was as sharp as a hawk in figuring these things out."

Caroline grinned. "That must have frightened your brothers."

"It did. I'd let our mother know, and this aggravated them all the more. But they weren't the ones doing all the cooking and cleaning, so it didn't bother them if Mother and I had to do it."

"Good for you. They should have behaved more like gentlemen."

Allie nodded in agreement. "It was their own fault for misbehaving."

"You have my deep admiration, Allison Martin."

Allie took a moment to let her new last name sink in. Allison Martin. Allie Martin. Mrs. Travis Martin. She rolled the name around in her mind and smiled. It fit. It fit very well indeed.

***

"Sheriff, Ida's at it again."

Eric was in the middle of settling a dispute between Hank and Wilber over tree branches that were hanging over Hank's property when he heard the person call out to him. "Excuse me," he told the two men. He turned to face a very irate Jerry. "What's this about Ida?"

"She came by my house again to tell my wife that I'm having an affair," Jerry snapped. "I thought you put a stop to this nonsense."

With a glance at Hank and Wilber, he said, "I'll be back to talk about the tree." Urging Jerry to walk down a secluded path with him, he told him, "I put Ida in jail for an entire week."

"Maybe you should put her away for good."

"Come now, Jerry. You know I can't do that. Besides, the judge has already talked to me about putting her in jail in the first place. I can't do that again."

"Well, you need to do something. She's ruining my reputation. I'm the school superintendent. Do you know how bad this makes me look?"

"We all know Ida makes up stories about people. You remember what she did to my wife, don't you? Some of the townsfolk still believe those things Ida said about Caroline."

Jerry stopped and turned to face him. "That's the problem. There are some who believe Ida. Now every time I go somewhere, I can see they're wondering if I'm running off to spend time with another woman."

Well, that would cause a problem. Eric rubbed the back of his neck as he thought over the things he could do. So far, everything he had tried just hadn't worked. Ida was surprisingly resistant to learning anything. Who knew a woman could be so set in her ways?

"If you don't stop Ida, I will," Jerry added.

"I'm open to ideas if you got them," Eric replied.

"If you won't put her in jail, then send her to another town."

"I don't know if I can ask Mike to do that. He's got a good business here, and it's not easy to move ten children."

Jerry's jaw clenched. "You know what your problem is? You're weak. You're the sheriff. You need to make things happen. People around here obeyed the last sheriff. If you did more of the things he did, I bet that would put Ida in her place."

"The last sheriff wasn't a fair man," Eric argued. "He took bribes and let people get away with lawless behavior. This place wasn't safe when he was here."

"You think this place is safe? Abe Thomas would have gotten shot if he hadn't taken measures to protect himself, Ida won't stop spreading lies about people, and Carl got away with killing his wife."

"First of all, I'm not convinced Carl did it. Second, this place is safer than it was before I took over. There used to be duels right in the middle of the streets. Men would get drunk and harass the women in town without paying the consequences for it. People had to carry a gun wherever they went or risk getting robbed." He paused, then added, "And this all happened in broad daylight."

"Well, I demand you take care of things with Ida, or I'll find a reason to get a new sheriff in this town. Unlike you, I grew up with these people. My word carries more weight than yours does."

Eric sighed as he watched Jerry storm off. That didn't go well. No matter how he handled it, it probably wouldn't have gone well. How was he supposed to make Ida stop gossiping? He might as well be asked to make the sky turn dark in the middle of the day.

"I can't work miracles," he muttered.

With a shake of his head, he went back to Hank and Wilber, thankful that their senseless debate was much easier than handling a woman bent on gossiping.

And he didn't feel like tackling the issue today. Up to now, all his lectures hadn't made a difference. And it wasn't like Ida hadn't already been telling people Jerry was having an affair. Not that anyone believed her. Everyone knew she couldn't be trusted. So really, Jerry was worried over nothing.

No, he would wait until tomorrow after he had time to think over what he might say that would finally make Ida understand why spreading rumors was bad.

Chapter Sixteen

Allie glanced at the bed that evening and then picked up her pocket watch. It was almost ten o'clock, and she had yet to get into her nightclothes. After she and Travis had shared breakfast and supper together, was he really going to spend another night in the building?

Well, if she had to go out there to eat with him, then maybe she had to go out there to sleep with him, too. This was getting to be silly, after all. They were husband and wife, and it was time they acted like it.

Steeling her resolve, she lifted the kerosene lamp and left the cottage. The sun had already set, and she cursed herself for waiting so long. The distance from the cottage to the building had seemed like a short one during the day. Now, with the trees hovering over most of the cottage and the vines creeping up the building, the moonlight cast ominous shadows everywhere.

No wonder she had trouble sleeping at night. Even if Travis was a normal man, this place had a spooky feel to it.

With a shiver, she hurried to the building, grasping the kerosene lamp tighter lest she drop it by mistake. This time, she didn't bother knocking on the door. She flung the door open and ran inside, relieved when she shut the door behind her. Good. She'd made it unscathed.

"Is something wrong?" Travis called out.

She turned in time to see him bolting up in his makeshift bed and throwing his hat on.

"No. I got spooked, that's all," she assured him.

"Spooked? By what?" He headed over to one of the guns lining the wall.

"Nothing. It was just my imagination. It was silly." With a chuckle, she added, "I saw things in the shadows that weren't really there. It's my brothers' fault. They used to tell me scary stories. I enjoyed them at the time, but once in a while, I'll remember one of them and get spooked."

He relaxed and turned his back on the guns. "Why are you here? Do you need something?"

"Well," she took a deep breath, "now that you mention it, I do. I'd like for you to come to bed with me."

His jaw dropped. "What?"

"We ate our meals together. I thought we should sleep together, too."

"But, but…" After a moment, he gestured to his bed. "That's too small to fit both of us."

"We can sleep in the cottage. That bed fits us just fine."

He didn't make a move to the door, so she remained in her spot, not willing to budge from this any more than she'd been willing to eat alone. Her ploy had worked very well for the meals. Though he hadn't said much, she sensed they were drawing closer. And maybe it was best to do this all at once. If they had one full day to be a normal, married couple, then it might be like removing a thorn from the flesh. Difficult at first but healing faster.

"Well," he glanced at the door, "I don't know."

"We don't have to do anything," she said. "We can just sleep like we did when Ida was here."

"I didn't get any sleep that night," he whispered as he turned away from her.

It took her a moment to understand what he meant. Her mother had warned her about being proper at all times around men while she was on her way to this territory.

"Once a man gets a certain thought in his mind, he's likely to go through with it," her mother had warned as she helped Allie pack. "The best thing you can do is not be caught alone with one at any time. Make sure you stay in public until you marry Eric Johnson. He's the only one who'll have the right to be alone with you."

Had Travis entertained thoughts of an intimate nature while they had shared the bed together? And if so, why hadn't he acted on it? She wouldn't have refused him. He was her husband. He had every right to be with her that way.

The answer, of course, was obvious. He hadn't acted on his thoughts because he was too shy. It was hard enough to get him to share a meal with her, let alone consummate their marriage.

Never in a million years did Allie think she'd have to be the one to initiate that part of their marriage, but by the way he ran over to the kitchen table and grabbed a brush and paint, she realized if they were ever going to move onto the next stage in their marriage, she was going to have to take the lead.

"Travis, this is silly," she said. "You can't mean to work all night. I'm your wife. I'm more than happy to do whatever you want in the bed."

***

Travis paused, but only for a second. She was a virgin. She didn't know what she was saying. She had no idea what he wanted to do.

He took an uneasy breath, noting the way his hands shook as he removed the lid to the paint. It was all he had to do to the table and then he'd be finished with it. After this, he could work on the chairs she wanted for outside. He dipped the brush into the paint.

"I wish you wouldn't feel the need to avoid me," she said, setting the kerosene lamp in the corner of the room.

He heard her footsteps as she made her way over to him, and he dropped the brush into the container. He made a move to pull it out when her hand covered his. He might have knocked the container over had she not caught it.

"We're married, Travis," she whispered. "It's alright to do this."

She took the container and set it aside, placing the lid back on it and setting the brush on the towel so it would dry. He took a step away from her. It wasn't that he didn't want to do what she had in mind. He just couldn't believe he was understanding her correctly. What woman in her right mind would want to be with him that way?

She approached him, and he took another step back until his backside hit the table. He was ready to stop her when she stood up on her tiptoes and leaned into him. Though she couldn't have intended to let her breasts brush against him, that was exactly what happened, and the sensation made him freeze in place.

She took off his hat and threw it on the table. Then she smiled and said, "That's better. I like being able to look into your eyes. You have such a lovely blue color. I can't recall a time when I ever saw a blue so bright on anyone."

He studied her expression, just to make sure she was being sincere. It wasn't his experience to receive compliments about the way he looked. Yes, he'd received compliments on his fine craftsmanship, but that was for things he created with his hands. But as for himself, he hadn't had anything worth noting.

Until now. Because he could tell she was being sincere. His heart warmed. It was nice to be told there was something attractive about him, even if that something was as simple as his eye color.

She wrapped her hand around his neck and pulled him toward her. Her eyes closed, and she parted her mouth, inviting him to kiss her. As much as he was afraid to do it, he was too curious to pull away. Just what was it like to share a kiss? He'd seen people kiss, and they seemed to enjoy it. It'd be nice if he could do it, too. He'd like to partake in something that was common to the human experience.

Closing his eyes, he let his mouth touch hers and was rewarded with a spark of pleasure as it coursed through him. It was similar to the way he felt when she touched him, except this was better than the time she held his hand. Because this particular act aroused him.

He ended the kiss, his face warm. He was certain she hadn't meant to stir up the kind of thoughts he was now having because he unwittingly recalled how she looked without clothes on, and she didn't even know he'd seen her change into her nightshirt that night they were in the bedroom. She'd thought he was asleep.

"I won't do this if you really don't want to," Allie said. "Would you like me to leave?"

He should say yes. If he wanted to do what was best for her, he'd tell her to go back to the cottage. But he couldn't say the words. Not when his arms refused to push her away. And not when she continued to hold him and look up at him as if she wanted to stay with him.

After a long moment, he shook his head. No. He didn't want her to leave. He wanted her to stay. More than that, he wanted to kiss her again.

As if she could read his mind, she encouraged him to lower his head and kiss her. This kiss wasn't as awkward as the first one. This time, he knew what to expect, and he noted how soft her lips were. She didn't seem to mind kissing him. That was a promising sign. Growing up, he had assumed he'd never share such a moment with a woman. But it was nice to finally be able to do it. Well, it was more than nice. It was, by far, the most exciting thing that had ever happened to him.

He thought she might pull away at some point during this kiss, but she didn't. Instead, she parted her mouth and brushed her tongue along his bottom lip. Another spark shot through him, making him hesitate. Just what should he do? Was it a good idea to give into the urge to accept her into his mouth? If he did that, then he'd have even more thoughts of things he'd like to do to her, and he wasn't sure she'd be all that happy about them.

She ran her hands down his arms and then wrapped her arms around his waist, pulling him closer to her. Whether she had intended it or not, this allowed his erection to press up against her, and this compelled him to accept her into his mouth. From there, he proceeded to interlace his tongue with hers. Now, this kind of kiss was much better because it helped to relax him.

He supposed some things were guided by instinct. People didn't have to be told to do them. They just naturally did them as the situation called for it. This seemed to be one of those situations because, without consciously thinking of it, his hands went to her breasts, cupping them in his hands.

In his mind, he recalled the way they'd looked in the mirror as she undressed in front of it. They were perfectly round with pink buds in the center. It was these buds that he felt as he brushed over her breasts. He wasn't sure, but he thought they hardened as he continued to caress them.

She shivered, and for a moment, he thought he'd done something to repulse her. He immediately drew back, fully expecting her to run out of the building, but instead, she started to unbutton her shirtwaist.

He couldn't move. He couldn't even breathe. Was he dreaming? Had he fallen asleep while painting the kitchen table?

Surely, this couldn't really be happening. Not to him. And not with someone as beautiful as her.

She shrugged off her shirtwaist and then pulled the chemise over her head, exposing those wonderful breasts he'd been unable to get out of his mind since he first saw them. It was much better to see her face to face instead of looking at her reflection.

As she draped the clothes over a chair, he debated whether or not he should wake up. If this was a dream, why fight it? But then, he couldn't be dreaming because never, in a million years, had his dreams ever taken this turn. If he was dreaming, she'd either be laughing at him or afraid of him.

Swallowing the lump in his throat, he watched as she removed the rest of her clothes. No. This couldn't be happening. Not really happening. It had to be a dream. A very unusual dream, but a dream nonetheless.

When she finished placing her things on the chair, she returned to him, her fingers on the top button of his shirt. "Don't you want to make love to me?"

His gaze lowered to her fingers. Did he want to make love to her? In his entire life, he couldn't think of anything he'd ever wanted more.

"I'm your wife, Travis," she whispered. "I want to be with you in every way a wife is supposed to be with her husband."

"I-" His voice cracked, so he cleared his throat. "I want to be with you, too." That took a lot of effort to say, and the only reason he managed it was because the male part of him was demanding he do it.

She smiled at him then, and he was assured that she was telling the truth, that she was sincere in wanting to consummate their marriage. Her gaze went to the buttons on his shirt as she unfastened them, taking her time as she did so. The process probably shouldn't have been so erotic. And maybe it wouldn't have been, except she was doing it with the intent of making love to him.

"The scars aren't only on my face. They're on my body, too," he warned. "When I was a child, I had varicella. It was so bad that I couldn't stop scratching. So, I'm not like other men."

She paused at the last button on his shirt and looked up at him. "I don't want you to be like other men. I want you to be who you are. And when I look at you, I see a caring and tender man who only wants the best for others. When we make love, that's the person I'm going to be with."

Then she loosened the last button and slid the shirt off his shoulders. Afterward, she slipped her hands beneath his undershirt and helped him take it off. He held his breath as she studied his chest, running her hands along his skin, not shying away when she came across the scars.

"You're strong," she whispered as she traced the muscles in his arms. "I find that very attractive."

Then she lowered her hands to his denims. He finally released his breath. She wasn't repulsed by him. She'd taken a good look at him, even touched a couple of the scars, and she hadn't shown any indication that he repulsed her. More than that, she was still willing to make love to him.

He helped her with the buttons on his denims and took off the rest of his clothes. He noted the slight trembling in his hands. Even if she hadn't balked at the scars, he still couldn't help but be nervous about where this was heading. He wanted to return to that state of mind where his fears had abated, where instinct had taken over and allowed him to gather the courage to touch her breasts. The pause in touching her had been enough to make him hesitate again.

But as she reached down to touch his penis, he started to relax. Her touch was gentle, as if she wasn't certain of what she was doing, and he remembered this wasn't only his first time—it was hers, too. Except, she wasn't letting her insecurities prevent her from exploring him.

Taking a deep breath, he brought his hands back to her breasts and cupped them. He focused on her nipples, curious at the way they grew hard as he brushed them with his thumbs. It was much like the way he hardened as she traced the length of him with her fingers. And in many ways, the fact that she was so intimately exploring him helped him forget about his scars.

Her hand cupped around his penis, and he moaned. It was much better than when he did it.

She glanced up at him. "Did I hurt you?"

"No," he said, his voice soft. "It felt good."

"What you're doing is making me feel good, too," she replied, blushing as she made her confession.

He noted that she was as nervous as he was, and he suddenly didn't feel so awkward. They were both learning what lovemaking entailed. Neither had been with another person this way. And that being the case, perhaps he didn't have to worry about every little thing he was doing. If he didn't do things perfectly, how would she know?

Encouraged, he lifted her up and put her on the table, eager to get a better look at her. He took a moment to study her body. She was flawless of course. There wasn't a single thing wrong with her. He couldn't have done a better job if it'd been up to him to create her.

"I've never seen anything more beautiful in my whole life," he told her.

Then, before she could respond, he leaned forward and kissed her, this time not hesitating to brush his tongue along hers. She wrapped her arms around him and deepened the kiss. He ran his hands over her body, taking his time to further explore her, wishing to sear the memory of her into his mind forever.

When he reached the area between her legs, she let out a low moan and spread them further apart. He traced the curls with his fingers before touching the folds of her flesh. He went lower and realized she was wet. Curious, he put a finger into her, wondering what she felt like. The warm folds of her flesh wrapped around him. This was where his penis would soon be, and he honestly couldn't think of anything else that'd feel better than this.

The last of his nerves settling down, his mouth left hers, and he kissed her cheek, then her neck, and then went lower. She shifted back, giving him better access to her breasts, and he brought his mouth to the pink bud that beckoned to him.

She whispered his name and lifted her hips, prompting his finger to slide deeper into her. Excited, he slid in another finger. She rewarded him with a groan and began rocking her hips, a movement that aided him in the process of stroking her core.

His mouth left her breast and went to the area between her legs. She laid back on the table and spread her legs further, giving him the perfect opportunity to study her. She was beautiful. So absolutely beautiful. And to think he had the pleasure of enjoying her for the rest of his life.

Her hands gripped his shoulders, and she murmured how much she was enjoying what they were doing. He brought his mouth to her sensitive nub and kissed it. She let out gasp and cried out for him to do it again. Intrigued, he did as she wished, and noting the way her flesh clenched around his fingers, he brushed the nub with his tongue. She asked him to do it again, and he obliged, eager to do whatever he could to give her as much pleasure as possible.

Fortunately, she wasn't the least bit shy in letting him know what she liked. He explored different techniques in stroking her with his tongue until he found the one that made her moan the loudest. He continued his ministrations until she let out a final cry and stilled, her body jerking in time with the clenching and unclenching of her core.

When she relaxed, she murmured that she wanted him to enter her. More than excited, he rose above her and slid into her. There was a moment of resistance, where he had to pass through her virginal barrier. And at first he thought he'd hurt her, but then she wrapped her legs around his waist and pulled him deeper into her.

"Don't stop," she whispered. "Make me your wife."

With a moan, he pulled halfway out and then went back in, noting the ease with which he did so. He repeated the movement, taking a moment to study her expression. She let out a contented sigh and smiled at him. Good. He definitely wasn't hurting her.

He closed his eyes and continued making love to her. The pleasure building up within him insisted he give into his release, but he'd slow down at times just to delay it. At times, he even opened his eyes and focused on something in the room. He wasn't in any hurry to climax. This was, by far, the best thing that had ever happened to him, and he fully intended to enjoy every moment of it.

Eventually, however, his body refused to delay the inevitable, and he ended up giving into the need to reach the peak. He cried out her name and grew still as his seed filled her core. Wave after wave of pleasure crashed into him, making him feel better than he ever had in his life. And it was even better because Allie still had her legs wrapped around his waist, a silent message that she had fully accepted him. She'd been willing to share the most intimate activity one person could share with another, and for that, he loved her.

When he was spent, he leaned toward her and kissed her. "That was the best thing that ever happened to me," he whispered.

She brushed the hair out of his eyes and smiled. "It was the best thing that ever happened to me, too."

Returning her smile, he gave her another kiss, not in any hurry to end it. When his mouth left hers, he said, "Thank you for looking beyond my appearance."

She cupped his face in her hands. "When I look at you, I don't see the scars. I see the man that's really there, and you're handsome."

She meant it. He could tell that by the way she was looking at him. Whatever had he done to deserve her? Swallowing the lump in his throat, he said, "I love you, Allie."

"I love you, too."

They kissed for another couple minutes. He was in no rush to end this moment in his life. If only it would last forever. Because in this moment, he'd never been happier. Here, with her, he was normal. And more than that, he wasn't alone. No. With her, he was complete.

Chapter Seventeen

The next morning, Allie woke up before Travis did. After they finally consummated the marriage, he'd been much more willing to join her in their bedroom in the cottage. He had turned out to be a very considerate lover. Not that she'd doubted he would be since her mother had told her a man who treated a woman well outside the bed would treat her well in the bed, too.

But it still made her heart leap in excitement when she recalled his tenderness toward her. He loved her. He didn't have to come out and say it. She knew it in the way he'd touched and kissed her.

The best part was, he was still in the cottage with her. She thought she might have to try to convince him to go to bed with her, but fortunately, when she had asked him if he'd go to their bedroom, he had simply nodded and followed her to the cottage. She couldn't be sure if this was finally the turning point where he realized he was safe with her. Hopefully, it was. At least when she woke up that morning, he'd been in bed with her.

After she quietly dressed, she went to the kitchen to make breakfast. She decided to make pancakes that morning, and once she was done, she rinsed out the bowl.

As she turned to pour them both a cup of coffee, she was surprised to see Travis standing in the doorway, hat in hand, a shy smile on his face.

Well, he wasn't making a move to run off, so that was good. He was at least willing to eat this meal with her without being pinned down to do it.

"Have a seat," she greeted, waving him into the room. She put the plate of warm pancakes in the center of the table then set out their cups. "I hope you had a good night's sleep."

"As I recall, we didn't do much sleeping," he said as he settled into his chair.

She stared at him for a moment and then laughed. "Why, Travis, I believe you just made a joke."

He shrugged, his face growing pink.

"It was a good joke," she assured him. Then to show him she meant it, she kissed his cheek. "And I certainly didn't mind losing some sleep."

She didn't think the comment would make his blush deepen, but it did.

Deciding it might be best to turn the conversation to something that would make him more comfortable, she added, "I thought I'd work on the flowerbed today. I know it's late in the season, but all the work will get things ready for next year."

"I should check on Carl today and see how he's doing," Travis said. "When I come back, I want to paint the new table." He glanced around the room. "Now that the house looks nice, I want to have nicer furniture to go with it. It's amazing what you've done to this place."

She sat in her chair and smiled at him. "Thank you. I can't take all of the credit, though. Caroline and Phoebe helped."

"Is that what they were doing when they were here?"

She nodded as she put some pancakes on his plate. "We did some talking, too, but we were cleaning for the most part."

She jumped up and grabbed some syrup for him to put on his pancakes. "I almost forgot this."

"Caroline and Phoebe are nice women."

"They are. I'm glad I got a chance to meet them."

He poured some syrup on his pancakes then glanced at her. "You know, I like their husbands. Abe and Eric have always been nice to me."

He handed the syrup to her but didn't continue talking. She sensed he had something else in mind, so she encouraged, "What is it?"

"Well…" He picked up his fork and turned it over in his hand for several seconds before saying, "I was just thinking that since you get along with Phoebe and Caroline and I get along with Abe and Eric that maybe…" He cleared his throat. "Um, maybe we can have them over some time."

Not expecting this, she almost dropped the syrup as she was pouring it. "Really?"

"Growing up, I never had friends. It was just me and my father. I got the scars when I was five, and people made fun of me for it. Until I came here, there wasn't anyone I could trust not to make fun of me behind my back."

"Oh, Travis, that's awful."

He shrugged. "After a while, I didn't mind. I even liked being alone. It's easier to work with things than it is to deal with people." Shifting in his chair, he said, "I like being with you. You accept me as I am. When I'm with you, I feel like a normal person. I don't have to worry that you find me lacking."

"You're not lacking in anything."

"I know you mean that. I couldn't be sure with some in the past, but you're sincere. And because of that, you make me want to try new things. Caleb said Eric and Caroline have had supper with Abe and Phoebe. I thought it'd be nice if we could have all of them here whenever it's convenient for you."

"I think that's a wonderful idea, but are you sure you're comfortable with that?"

"I probably won't say much," he said. "But if I never take a risk, I might miss out on something worthwhile. I know that's true after marrying you. My life has never been better, and I'm not just saying that because you make the most delicious food I've ever tasted."

She grinned, pleased to note he'd told another joke. "My life is better with you, too."

He returned her smile and started eating his breakfast.

***

Eric walked up to Ida's house where the younger children were playing a game of tag in the yard. Ida was sitting in a chair on the porch, her ankle propped up on a pillow that rested on a wooden crate. He'd heard she had sustained an injury to her ankle when she was on Carl's property. Well, if nothing else had come from the injury, at least he knew she wouldn't be able to run off this time when he started talking.

"How's the ankle doing?" he asked as he pulled up the other chair and sat beside her.

She narrowed her eyes at him. "You didn't come here to ask about my ankle. You came to give me another lecture about my tendency to gossip. But I haven't been spreading any falsehoods."

"No?" He leaned toward her and lowered his voice so the children wouldn't overhear him. "Jerry talked to me yesterday, and he was upset."

"He only has himself to blame. If he hadn't sought out another woman's bed, he would be just fine right now."

Eric groaned. "Ida, how many times do I have to tell you to stop this nonsense?"

"You told me to stop gossiping. I did that. I even apologized to your wife and told other people I was wrong about her. And she wasn't the only one I was doing that for. I've been doing that for everyone I've spread lies about. But," she straightened in her chair and leaned toward him, "I will not apologize for warning a poor, unsuspecting woman that her husband is committing adultery. She has a right to know."

Eric shook his head in aggravation. "Just because you *think* Jerry is having an affair, it doesn't mean he is."

"That's just it, Sheriff. I don't *think* it. I know it." When he frowned at her, she continued, "Maybe you have to be a woman to understand, but we're born with an intuition that lets us know if something's wrong. Violet's been sensing something has been wrong for the past six months. She just couldn't tell what it was until I told her I caught Jerry hiding that green dress in his wagon."

With a groan, Eric rubbed his eyes. "He already explained that. It was supposed to be a gift for-" Something in the back of his mind told him Ida had just let something very important slip into the conversation, and after a moment of sorting through her words, he knew exactly what it was. "What color did you say the dress was?"

"Green. It had buttons down the front, and it had little lacy frills around the edges of the sleeves. Violet wouldn't wear that kind of dress. It's not her style."

Eric's eyes grew wide. It couldn't be. It wasn't possible. He knew Jerry. Jerry was a good man. He was the superintendent of the school. He housed the preacher whenever he was in town, and he helped him with the sermons. He doted on his wife and children. The family always looked happy whenever they were together.

It didn't make sense. Why would Jerry want to kill anyone, much less Lydia? Then Eric recalled she'd been expecting a child. The doctor even said she'd been about five months along.

And Ida just said Violet noticed something was wrong for the last six months.

As much as he hated where his thoughts were going, a lot of the pieces fit. Violet had said Jerry went to dump off their garbage at the landfill outside of town the evening Lydia was murdered, and since Hank said he saw Jerry heading out in that direction with his wagon, Eric hadn't thought more of it than that.

But…what if he dropped off the garbage and then went to pick up Lydia? He would have been in a wagon, and she'd been pushed from a moving vehicle. That didn't explain why she changed into a red dress, but Eric would have to let that question wait for a while. At the moment, he had to focus on Jerry's motive. If Lydia had been carrying his child, it would do a lot of damage to his reputation.

And now, with Ida telling others he was having an affair, his secret was in danger of being exposed. Carl Richie wasn't attacked until Ida started that particular rumor. What if, in an act of desperation, Jerry was trying to coerce Carl into confessing to the murder? And what if, since Carl wasn't going to confess, Jerry got desperate enough to kill Carl, too?

Eric bolted to his feet. "I have something I need to do. Thanks, Ida."

Ida's jaw dropped, but she didn't say anything as he hurried off her property.

***

Travis picked up the gun from the top shelf in the building and put it in the holster around his waist. He put on his hat and started heading for the door when he caught sight of Allie from the window. She was taking a pail out to the well.

Just the sight of her was enough to make him stop. He still couldn't believe she'd made love to him. And not just once, but three times. Then she'd welcomed him to the kitchen table for breakfast and shared another meal with him. It was something a normal husband and wife would do. He no longer had to feel like an outcast. He now had a place where he belonged. And that place was with her.

He glanced at the box resting on the back shelf. After a moment, he went over to the shelf and took the box. He opened it up. All of Allie's notes were in there, right along with his father's pipe, the toy train, and his mother's wedding ring.

He picked up the ring and studied the gold band. His father had kept it in his pocket up to the day he died, saying it made him feel like Travis' mother was with him. Then, as he lay on his deathbed, he gave it to Travis. "Give it to the young lady you marry someday," his father had told him.

At the time, Travis hadn't had the heart to tell his father that he'd never have anyone to give it to. Instead, he'd assured his father that he would and left it at that because he hadn't wanted to ruin his father's last moments on things that would never be.

But he had gotten married. Granted, it happened in a way he never would have expected. As his father often told him, sometimes good things happened when people least expected it. And he couldn't think of anything better than having Allie in his life. For the first time in his life since his father died, he had someone who could accept him—really accept him.

Sure, Abe and Eric did. Carl even did, too. They treated him with respect. But it was different with her. She had let him in her heart. She was willing to make a life with him as his wife, and she was willing to have his children. That made her special in a way no one else could ever be.

He glanced at the window and saw Allie was returning to the cottage with the pail. She was worth giving the ring to. He shut the box and put it back on the shelf. Clasping the gold band in his hand, he left the building and followed her into the cottage. She had just put the pail on the worktable when she noticed him.

"Do you think you'll be back in time for lunch?" she asked.

"Probably not," he replied. "The ride to Carl's will take about an hour."

Though she smiled, he noted the disappointment in her eyes. "I didn't realize it took that long to go out there. So when do you think you'll be back?"

"If all goes well, a couple hours."

She dipped a cup into the pail and filled it with water. "You should have something to drink before you leave." She lifted the cup and held it to him.

As he took it, his fingers brushed hers and, once again, that familiar tingle raced up and down his spine. This time, he didn't find it unnerving. It was a nice reminder of the previous evening.

"I know this is going to sound silly since a couple of hours isn't really that long," she said as he drank the water, "but I'm going to miss you."

He stopped drinking just shy of emptying the cup, his eyes meeting hers. She was going to miss him? He couldn't recall anyone ever missing him before.

Setting the cup down, he closed the distance between them and opened his free hand to show her the ring. "This was my mother's. I thought you might like to wear it. You know, because you're my wife." He cleared his throat, suddenly feeling a bit of his former shyness returning. "Um, I can adjust the size so it'll fit."

"You want me to wear your mother's ring?" Allie asked, the tone in her voice letting him know she was touched by his offer.

"Well, you're the most important person in my life, and the ring is one of the few things I have that mean something to me. I'd like you to have it."

Tears filled her eyes as she accepted it. "Travis, that's such a beautiful thing for you to say. I'll be happy to wear it. In fact, I won't ever take it off."

"Well, we need to see if it fits first."

After she brushed away her tears, she slipped it on her finger, and he noted it was loose. Taking her hand in his, he judged how loose it was. "When I come back, I'll make it smaller so it fits better."

"In the meantime, do you mind if I keep it in my pocket?"

"No, I don't mind at all."

She slipped it into her pocket and stood up on her tiptoes to kiss him. He brought her into his arms and deepened the kiss. He didn't know if his father or mother could look down from heaven to see them, but if they could, he imagined they were smiling, knowing the ring was with someone deserving of it. More than that, they would be happy he'd found someone who sincerely cared for him, and that made his joy all the more complete.

Chapter Eighteen

Carl glanced at his gold panning supplies. He shouldn't be stuck inside his cabin. He should be at the stream seeing if he could find gold. If his father hadn't been so certain there was a good amount of gold somewhere along the twenty acres, Carl would have given up a long time ago. But his father had been certain of it.

He stared at the missive he was writing to Juliet Gilbert. Not many women were answering mail-order bride ads, so he considered himself fortunate she had. At the rate he was going, he would need another five years to cover the portion of the stream he hadn't panned yet. In order to have that much time, he needed to get the child, and to have one, he needed to have a wife.

He let out a shaky breath. He didn't know what prospect frightened him more: having to get the wife pregnant or risk being killed by Lydia's murderer. Both seemed equally unpleasant.

He rose from the small desk and studied the land. He lived on the slope of a hill, and that hill was covered with trees. Thick ones. Anyone could be out there, and he wouldn't know it.

But he had to get to town and mail off the missive to Juliet tomorrow. That's when the next stagecoach was coming in. If the killer was out there, he supposed he'd just have to deal with him. He let out a heavy sigh and returned to the missive so he could finish it.

After he was done, he addressed the envelope and sealed it up. A knock at the door made him bolt upright. Who'd be knocking on his door? Was it the killer?

As soon as the thought came to mind, he dismissed it. That was ridiculous. The killer wouldn't come right up to his door and knock. He'd be lying in wait for him and tackle him to the ground like he did last time.

To be sure, though, he peaked out the window to see who it was. Travis stood at the door. He relaxed and went to answer it.

"I wanted to make sure you're alright," Travis greeted.

"I'm doing as well as can be expected," Carl replied.

"You're still not getting much sleep?"

"It's hard to sleep when you know someone wants you dead."

"Maybe you should come over to my place. It's not doing you any good to stay here by yourself."

Carl considered the offer but hated the thought that the killer might come through his cabin and destroy the few things he cared about, his mother's oak desk being one of them. "I'll be fine as long as I stay inside."

Travis glanced at the small barn. "Are you feeding your horse?"

"Yes. It's about all I do outside."

"Is there anything you'd like me to do?"

"Well," he went over to the desk and took out the missive, "I would appreciate it if you'd take this to the stagecoach tomorrow." Recalling how self-conscious Travis was about his looks, he quickly amended, "On second thought, you don't have to."

"No, it's fine. I'll take it."

Carl studied him. "Are you sure?"

He nodded and held his hand out. "I'm sure."

Carl handed him the missive. "Thanks."

Travis took the missive but didn't leave.

"Is something wrong?" Carl asked.

Travis glanced around, and Carl followed his gaze, wondering if there was something Travis had picked up on that he had missed.

"I don't know if I should say anything," Travis said, his voice low, "but it's been on my mind ever since the sheriff told me."

"What is it?"

"Did you know Lydia was expecting a child?"

Lydia was what?

"I take it by your expression, you didn't," Travis said. "The sheriff had her body dug up and asked the doctor to do a thorough examination. She was five months along."

"Well, the child wasn't mine. I only managed to get her into bed at the end of June." And that had taken a lot out of him. Just thinking about it drained him. "Before then, we hadn't done anything for three years."

"Then the sheriff might be right. Whoever killed her wanted to keep the pregnancy a secret."

It also explained why Lydia kept laughing at him and saying that he'd never get the child he needed in order to hold onto the stream. She'd only allowed him to be in bed with her so she could remind him of how inept he was. It was just another way to make him miserable. If the killer wasn't after him, he'd be inclined to thank the man for getting rid of her.

"If you can think of anyone who might be the father, it'd help the sheriff narrow down the suspects."

Carl snorted. "She slept with so many men even I lost track of them all." And she hadn't been shy about telling him all about her escapades while in town, either.

"Well, it might help to write them down anyway. I can give the sheriff the list for you."

He didn't see how it'd do any good, but since Travis seemed to want him to say yes, he said, "I'll think about it. Going over a list of my dead wife's lovers isn't exactly something I want to do."

"I understand, but if you can give the sheriff anything to help him catch the killer, it'd be worth the unpleasantness you'd have to go through."

"I'll think about it," he repeated. After a moment, he added, "Thanks for delivering that letter for me."

Travis tucked the missive into his pocket and tipped his hat.

Carl gave one last look around his property as Travis got up on his horse. Nothing seemed to be out of the ordinary. But then, nothing had seemed unusual that day he was attacked at the stream, either. With a shiver, he closed the door.

He went over to the chair and looked out the window as Travis headed off his land. Sometimes he envied Travis. All of his scars were on the surface. Carl had to carry his around inside.

With a sigh, he leaned back and stared at the wall in front of him. What had once been a home was now a prison. Maybe he should let the murderer kill him. At least then, his worthless life would be over with.

A noise on the porch caught his attention. Bolting out of the chair, he looked out the window and saw a dog sniffing around the front door. His eyebrows furrowed. He hadn't seen that dog before. Sure, a stray would come through here once in a while, but this large brown and white dog hadn't been one of them.

He opened the door, and the dog sat down, looked up at him, and whined. Surprised, he knelt in front of the animal and patted its head. The dog wagged its tail. The dog wasn't wild. By the looks of it, it was used to being around humans.

"Where did you come from?" Carl asked, scratching the dog behind its ears.

The dog panted in response, seeming to smile at the attention.

"You've got to be one of the most docile dogs I've ever seen," he murmured. "I wonder where your owner is."

The dog, of course, had no way of telling him.

"Well, maybe your owner will come looking for you. In the meantime, you can stay here." He waved the dog in, but the dog remained seated. "Come in. Come on, girl."

The dog stayed in place.

How could he encourage the dog to come in? After a moment, he went over to the container resting on the shelf above his potbelly stove and took out a piece of jerky. He showed it to the dog.

"Are you hungry?" he asked.

The dog sauntered into the cabin and stopped in front of him. It sat down then got up on its hind legs.

"Whoever you belong to did a good job of training you," he said as he broke off a piece of the jerky and fed the animal. "You're clean, too." He petted the dog and smiled. "You know, it's been a long time since anything good was in this place."

He gave the dog the rest of the jerky, and the dog was more than happy to eat it.

Something hard pressed into the back of Carl's head, and he froze. A metal click let him know he was on the receiving end of a gun. He cursed his foolishness. He never should have turned his back on the open door!

"Ginger," the man behind Carl whispered to the dog, "leave."

The dog whined for a moment but then turned and left the cabin.

"Now," the man whispered in Carl's ear, "I've had enough of waiting. Get over to that desk and write a letter confessing to Lydia's murder."

Carl tried to glance over his shoulder to see who was behind him, but the man struck him on the side of the head with the butt of the gun. Wincing, Carl cried out and touched the fresh wound. When he inspected his fingers, he saw blood on them.

After a moment, Carl steeled his resolve and straightened up to his full height. He was tired of quivering in fear, and he was tired of fighting the inevitable. Of all the things he'd done in his life to mess it up, confessing to a murder he didn't commit wasn't going to be one of them.

"Do what you have to do," he told the man behind him, "but I'm not writing that letter."

The man swore, and this time Carl made out who it was. Jerry Conner. Somehow being able to put a voice with a face emboldened him to act. He swung around and punched Jerry across the jaw. The gun went off, and Carl went to the floor, sure he'd been hit. But the absence of pain let him know Jerry had missed.

From outside, the dog started barking, and Carl scrambled to his feet, searching for something—anything—he could use as a weapon. He found a letter opener on the desk and turned to face Jerry. He would have lunged at Jerry had Jerry not been pointing the gun at him.

The two stood still. Both staring at the other. Carl's fist tightened around the letter opener. Maybe if he threw it and ducked, he could catch Jerry by surprise.

The dog stepped into the cabin and barked in Jerry's direction. Jerry glanced at the dog, and Carl took that as his cue. He threw the letter opener, aiming for Jerry's forehead. Then he ducked.

Jerry, however, also ducked. And worse, another gunshot rang through the air, followed by shattering glass. Carl squeezed his eyes, fully expecting a bullet to hit him. But it didn't. Parting his eyes enough so he could see his body, he noticed he was fine. Then he opened his eyes all the way and looked over at Jerry, thinking for sure Jerry would be standing right over him.

But Jerry was face first on the floor, a pool of blood beneath him. Glancing at the back of Jerry's head, Carl saw the bullet wound.

The dog went over to Jerry and sniffed him, whining as it did so.

"It's alright," came Travis' voice.

Carl glanced over at the doorway as Travis and Eric came into the cabin.

"We didn't want to risk shooting you," Eric said, "so we had to wait until we had a clear view of him."

Shaking, Carl asked, "How did you know he was here?"

"I thought I saw someone coming on this property on my way here," Travis said, "so I pretended to leave and kept watch until I saw Jerry and the dog. I followed them up here and waited to see what would happen." He pointed to Eric. "He happened to meet up with me along the way."

"Ida found Jerry with Lydia's dress," Eric said. "He was hiding it in his wagon. I've searched his wagon. It's not there anymore. My guess is that he burned it, and since Ida wouldn't stop talking about the affair he was having, he got desperate and made another attempt to pin the murder on you."

Carl released his breath, unaware he'd been holding it.

"It's going to be alright," Eric told him. "The important this is you don't have to worry about him anymore."

"I've never been through anything like this before," Carl said.

"You'll be shaken up for a while, but things will calm down."

"I'm just glad we got here in time," Travis added.

"If only every incident ended so well," Eric agreed, slipping the gun in his holster.

Carl didn't understand it. He'd heard of Jerry. Even seen him when he was in town on occasion. His wife had the reputation as a good and faithful spouse. Why would he have an affair with Lydia?

"My list wouldn't have done any good," Carl told Travis. "I didn't know about Jerry."

"As much as I hate to admit it," Eric began, "I'm glad Ida didn't keep her mouth shut. I didn't think Jerry was capable of such a thing."

"Yeah, well, it's hard to know anyone," Carl replied. "People are good at pretending to be something they aren't when they want to keep a secret."

After a long moment of silence, the three men loaded Jerry onto Carl's wagon and took the body into town.

***

"I'm sorry," Eric told Violet later that day in her parlor while Ida watched her two children.

Violet wiped the tears from her eyes. "I knew something was wrong. I just didn't want to admit it."

"I wish I didn't have to bring you such bad news. No woman wants to think her husband is an adulterer and a murderer."

She took a deep breath and released it. "How much will the others in town know about this?"

"Right now, it's just me, Travis, and Carl who know the truth, and we can be discreet. You don't have to worry the details will be exposed."

After a moment, she set her handkerchief on her lap, her gaze meeting his. "It's not me I worry about. I can handle the rumors. I just worry about my children. They're only eight and six."

From beside her, her dog rested its head on her leg and peered up at her. One thing Eric admired about dogs was their loyalty to their owners, even when the owners didn't deserve it.

"I know this is painful for you to talk about," Eric said, his voice soft, "but something has been bothering me. I was wondering if you could shed some light on it."

Petting Ginger, she asked, "What do you want to know?"

"When Lydia saw me before she was murdered, she had on that green dress Ida saw your husband hiding in the wagon. By the time I found her dead body, she was wearing red. Do you have any idea why she might have changed into a dress that wasn't hers?"

"Jerry's favorite color was red. Maybe she put it on to please him."

He nodded slowly, hoping she would pick up on the fact that he wasn't fully convinced.

"You think there might be another reason?" she asked.

"I think the dress being his favorite color might have been part of it. He took her far enough out of town that it would have taken us months to find her if a couple of women hadn't been taking a walk out that way. Anyone on a horse would have missed her because she was too far into the ravine to see from that angle. And if someone was in a carriage, they wouldn't be able to see her, either."

"I don't understand. What are you getting at, Sheriff?"

"I'm wondering if he might have had her change into a dress she didn't own in the hopes that her body would be so decayed no one would have recognized her. It was no secret Lydia was miserable. If we hadn't found her body, we might have assumed she ran off to another town just to get away from her husband."

"Yes. Probably."

"That leaves another question, though."

"Oh?"

"Where would he get the dress? That dress fit Lydia perfectly, and when I talked to Carl while coming into town, he verified that Lydia didn't own any red dresses."

She glanced down at the dog, and in doing so, Eric knew he'd put her in a difficult position. This was the hard part. He liked Violet. He had liked Jerry, too. And he was going to have to do one of the toughest things he'd ever done during his entire time as sheriff.

He leaned forward in the chair, his elbows resting on his knees. "Violet, I know you didn't push Lydia off the wagon. Jerry did. But only a woman would know how to give a man a dress that would fit another woman."

Her lower lip trembled and a tear slid down her cheek.

"Since you didn't commit the actual murder, the judge will go easier on you," he softly said. "But since you helped Jerry, you still have to share your part of the guilt."

She swallowed and ran her hand along the dog's head. "He was only with Lydia once. It was almost six months ago, and he and I had had a fight. He went out to get drunk, and she happened to be riding her horse along a deserted path as he was walking out of town to clear his head. He said it was all a blur. That one thing led to another and before he knew it, they'd," she gulped, "been together."

He watched as she struggled to keep her composure, but her hands trembled while she wiped another tear from her cheek. He quickly handed her a handkerchief and waited for her to continue.

"He told me right away," she said. "He was so ashamed, and I was so angry. He'd been faithful all these years in our marriage, and I had no reason to think he'd do anything with the town whore." She wiped more tears away. "I tried to forget it, to put it out of my mind. We tried to put that night away from us, but a month ago, Lydia told him she was expecting his child. She threatened to expose the affair if Jerry didn't give her money and take her out of town so she could start a new life elsewhere."

She took a deep breath then released it. "If it hadn't been for the timing of the conception, we wouldn't have worried about the threat, but Jerry panicked. We stood to lose everything, and we didn't have enough money to get her started on a new life in another town."

"So," she continued, "we came up with the plan to get rid of her. The dress was my idea. If someone happened to see him taking her out of town, we could claim it was me. He had her wear a bonnet that covered her face. He said he was taking her to the next town and would give her money for a ticket to go anywhere she wanted."

She took a shaky breath.

"The plan was for him to push her out of the wagon so she'd fall down the ravine," she added. "Then he was supposed to go back the next night and bury her. We were too afraid someone would find him if he lingered out there too long. We didn't think anyone would find her in only one day. He'd been careful to push her off at the right spot."

All the missing pieces had fallen into place, and now Eric could put this murder to rest. "I know that was hard for you," he replied, thinking over how much guilt she'd been carrying around with her all this time. "And I know this is going to be difficult, but we have to tell the judge." He rose to his feet and waited for her to get up.

She remained sitting for a couple minutes, just petting the dog and crying. But then, she stood up, sniffed back more tears, and wiped her face dry. "Sheriff, if it was just me, I could handle anything the judge wants to do with me. My concern is for the children. Do they have to know the details?"

"No, no they don't. We can tell people you needed to take care of a sick relative in another state and that you'll be back when the relative gets better. We'll tell your children the same thing. I have a feeling Ida won't have any problems keeping the secret since we're doing this for your children."

"Thank you," she replied.

In silence, he took her by the arm and led her to the door.

Chapter Nineteen

The next day, Allie took a break from weeding the flowerbed so she could bring Travis a glass of lemonade, thinking it would do more to quench his thirst than a hot cup of coffee would. When she stepped into the building, she saw that he was working on the coffin.

"The kitchen table and chairs were better projects," she said as she walked over to him.

He glanced up at her. "It's a good reminder that life's short. I can't help but think of my own mortality every time I'm asked to make a coffin or burn a body."

"Do you do that often?"

"More often than I want to." He put down his carving knife and accepted the lemonade. "In the past when I did this, I used to think my life had no purpose. I mean, beyond giving people scraps of junk to use or making things like furniture. And I suppose someone has to take care of people when they die, even as gruesome as the task is."

"Everything you do is necessary. You do have a purpose."

"Yes, I suppose I always did. But now that I have you, I have a reason to want to live."

On impulse, she stood up on her tiptoes and kissed him. "I'm glad to hear it. I want you to be around for a long time so we can enjoy many years together."

He smiled and lowered his head, ready to return the kiss, when they heard a horse neighing. His eyebrows furrowed, he took her hand and led her to the doorway. Her face flushed with pleasure. Now that he had opened up to her, he had no trouble showing her how much she meant to him. And that was nice.

When she saw that Eric was coming up to their property with two girls and a dog in the wagon, she glanced at Travis. "Does this have something to do with what happened yesterday?"

"Well, those are Jerry and Violet's daughters," Travis replied. "Carl took them over to Ida while Eric talked to Violet."

She didn't know much about what had happened, except that Jerry had been the one who murdered Lydia. Otherwise, the details eluded her, and she figured it was better that way. She didn't need to know them.

She followed Travis out to the clearing between the building and the cottage and waited for Eric to pull the wagon to a stop.

"Good afternoon," she called out.

Eric tipped his hat in greeting then helped the two girls down. The dog jumped down from the wagon and stood by the two girls.

"Should I get some lemonade to drink?" Allie asked.

The girls stood next to the wagon, their gazes going between Allie and Travis.

"Maybe in a moment," Eric said. "Girls, will you stay here while I talk to Mr. and Mrs. Martin?"

The oldest nodded and held her sister's hand.

Allie's heart went out to them. The poor things. They looked scared.

Eric came up to her and Travis. "Can we talk in there?" he gestured to the building.

"Sure," Travis replied.

Once they were in the building, Eric turned to Allie. "Did Travis tell you what happened yesterday?"

"Some of it," Allie slowly replied. "I know Jerry killed Lydia Richie."

"Yes, he did. And his wife, Violet, helped him. Violet will have to go to jail in a town north of here. The judge has decided she'll be there for five years. I promised Violet I wouldn't tell anyone else about her part in the murder. She doesn't want the children to know since they have to stay in this town." He paused and glanced out the window.

Allie followed his gaze and saw the oldest was trying to comfort the younger one who was wiping her eyes. The dog remained with them.

"The girls are Lilly and Janice," Eric said. "I told them and everyone else in town that their mother needs to visit a sick relative. It's bad enough they know what happened with their father. I don't see any reason they should have to know about their mother, too."

"I don't blame you," Allie replied. "They're going through a hard enough time as it is. But since you brought them here, do you want me and Travis to take care of them?"

"I know it's a lot to ask. I thought since you two are better isolated than anyone else, they stand the best chance of being protected from the talk in town. Even if they weren't the ones who killed Lydia, they'd have to put up with the stares and whispers. Some of the children might even harass them about it. I thought this would be the best place for them to get peace from all of that."

Allie glanced at Travis, wondering what he thought about it. If it was just her, the answer would be easy. She'd take them. But Travis was so shy around people. "What do you think?" she asked him.

Travis looked at the girls for a long moment, and she could tell he had mixed feelings about the proposition. Finally, he asked, "What do they think about us taking care of them?"

"To be honest, I didn't ask," Eric replied.

"We should ask," Travis said. "They're going through a hard enough time as it is. They shouldn't be stuck with someone who scares them."

Before either Eric or Allie could reply, he left the building. Curious, Allie followed him, Eric close behind.

When they reached the girls, Travis paused then took off his hat and knelt in front of them. "The sheriff would like you two and the dog to stay with me and my wife while your mother's gone." He glanced at Allie. "And that's fine with you?"

Allie nodded and smiled at the girls. "I'd be happy to have you and your dog here."

"I would, too," Travis added, turning back to them. "But it's important that you want to be here. I know I can seem scary. If you're afraid of me, we won't make you stay. I'm sure the sheriff can find another family for you to stay with instead."

"You don't scare us," the oldest said. "Aunt Ida said you're like Ginger." She patted the dog's head. "Big and friendly."

"But you aren't hairy," the youngest added.

"Aunt Ida didn't say he was hairy," the oldest told the younger one.

With a chuckle, Eric gestured to the oldest. "That one is Lilly. The younger one is Janice."

Travis ran his fingers over the edge of his hat for a moment then asked the girls, "My scars don't scare you?"

"I got a scar," Janice said and pulled the sleeve up her arm. "I fell off a chair when I was five."

Allie could tell that wasn't the response Travis expected, so she squeezed his shoulder. He glanced up at her, and she winked at him. Children, it seemed, were far more accepting of a person's imperfections than adults were.

"Well, as long as I don't scare you, we'll be more than happy to have you here," Travis said, turning back to the girls.

The girls nodded, and Eric clapped his hands. "Good. I was hoping this would work out. I think this will be something that will benefit everyone." He turned and shook Travis' hand. "Thank you."

"You're welcome," Travis replied.

Allie's gaze went to the girls. "Why don't we get some lemonade for you two and some water for Ginger? I bet you're all thirsty."

Lilly looked at her sister, who indicated her agreement. "Thank you, Mrs. Martin."

With a smile, she led them to the cottage while Eric and Travis continued talking.

***

A week later, Travis decided to take Allie and the girls to visit Abe and Phoebe. As he promised Lilly, he brought Ginger along, too. After losing their father and saying good-bye to their mother, they needed all the consolation they could get. The poor things were so young. There was no way they could understand the full scope of everything that had happened.

Janice moved over to him halfway during the trip and rested against him, as if to imply he made her feel safe. He glanced over at Allie, who smiled encouragingly at him. Still feeling awkward around children, he brought his arm around the girl's shoulders and gingerly patted her arm. The girl, in turn, sniffled and buried her face into his shirt.

Well, even if they didn't understand everything, they knew enough to know they'd lost their parents. Allie was holding Lilly, who was quiet. So maybe that was why Janice went over to him. Maybe she wanted someone to hold her, and Allie was comforting Lilly. Even if that was the case, he didn't mind doing his part to offer whatever he could to help the little girl. Loss was something he was familiar with. It was something he understood. It was something they had in common. And he could deal with that.

"I think you'll like Abe and Phoebe," Travis told the girls. "They're good people."

"We know. Papa liked Abe," Lilly said.

Travis' gaze met Allie's, and he caught the flicker of sorrow in her eyes. They were poor imitations of the girls' parents. But he reasoned they weren't supposed to replace their parents. Their job was to protect them and keep them safe until their mother could return. As for their father… He sighed and patted Janice's arm again. Well, there was no bringing him back. He and Allie would just do their best.

The horses led the wagon through the town, and once again, Travis noted the way the people stopped to turn and stare at them. Their attention didn't seem to be on him this time. No. This time, their interest seemed to be on the girls.

He pulled Janice closer and whispered, "You have nothing to be ashamed of. You understand?"

The girl nodded but sniffled, and he knew that as much as she wanted to believe him, a part of him couldn't help but think their stares were going to make her think she had some role to play in the death of Lydia, even though it wasn't true.

Irritated, he pulled the wagon to a stop, tilted his hat up, and gave them all a good look. "Don't you have anything better to do than stare at these innocent little girls?" he snapped.

Really, it was one thing for them to do it to him. He was an adult. He could take it. But he wouldn't tolerate them doing it to Lilly and Janice. If they were going to make life difficult for the girls, they would have to deal with him, and he wasn't going to back down like he had in the past.

The people must have seen the determination in his eyes since they lowered their gazes then and hurried on by. Assured they understood he wouldn't tolerate them treating the girls like they treated him, he snapped the reins, and the horses moved forward. Allie reached over and rubbed his arm in a way that indicated she was proud of him. He relaxed and focused his attention back to the road that would take them out of town and up to Abe's property.

The rest of the ride was spent in silence, except for the few times Ginger barked at a rabbit or squirrel along the tree-lined path that wound up to Abe's land. There was also the jingling of metal scraps, but Travis knew that was the alarm Abe had set up a while back to let him know when anyone was coming onto his property. He waited for the dog to bark this time, but Ginger only panted and studied her surroundings.

By the time they reached Abe's barn, Phoebe and her mother were coming out of the cabin to welcome them.

As soon as Travis pulled the wagon to a stop, the dog barked in excitement and jumped to the ground. She ran over to the two women and sniffed them.

Laughing, Phoebe petted the dog. "You sure are a playful thing," she said then scratched it behind the ears. Her gaze went to Travis and Allie. "I heard you're taking care of the Conner children."

"Yes," Travis replied as he set the brake. "They're Lilly and Janice." He gestured to each girl as he named her. "We thought it might be nice to bring them over."

"Well, we're happy to meet them," Phoebe's mother said, coming over to the wagon and giving them a warm smile. "Do you like peach tea? It's sweeter than regular tea."

"We haven't had peach tea before," Lilly replied.

"I think you'll like it," Allie told her.

Lilly and Janice glanced at each other and nodded. "Alright," Lilly said for both of them. "We'll try it."

Travis got down from the wagon and helped Janice, Lilly, and Allie down. "Where's Abe?" he asked Phoebe's mother.

"In the garden collecting some vegetables." Phoebe's mother glanced at the two girls. "You must miss your parents," she told them, her tone tender.

Lilly nodded and clasped Janice's hand.

"I know peach tea and cookies won't take the pain away," Phoebe's mother began, "but why don't we go into the cabin so you can have them?"

"That's a good idea," Travis said. "I'd like to talk to Abe." And it would be better if he could do it in private. The girls didn't need to hear what he had to tell him. He turned to Allie. "Do you mind staying with them while I do that?"

Allie smiled. "No, I don't mind." She squeezed his hand. "We'll be in the cabin."

He squeezed her hand in return before she and the other women led the girls into the cabin. This whole thing of Allie smiling and touching him in front of others was nice. It only affirmed that she wasn't ashamed of being with him. And that made them seem like even more of a normal couple. It was even better, though, since she wore his mother's ring. It hadn't taken long to get it resized so it fit her, and he was happy to note that she never took it off.

Heart light, he left the wagon and went to find Abe. As promised, Abe was in the garden. He had a basket by his feet with some food in it, but at the moment, Abe was pulling weeds away from one of the plants.

Travis also noticed the rifle next to him. "Are you expecting to shoot a gopher or rabbit?"

Abe tossed the weeds aside and glanced at him. "No. I carry the gun with me whenever I leave the cabin." He faced him and wiped the sweat from his brow. "I saw it was you as you came up, so I didn't bother leaving the garden."

"You saw me?"

Abe nodded and gestured behind Travis. "I got a good view of the path from here. I saw you before I heard the wagon trigger the metal pieces I bought from you."

Travis looked over his shoulder and saw a gap in the trees that did, indeed, give a good view of the path.

"What brings you out here?" Abe asked. "I didn't think you ever left your property."

"I thought I'd bring Allie and the girls out." He paused. "Since Phoebe's mother told the girls they must miss their parents, I'm assuming Eric came out here to tell you about Jerry and Violet Conner."

"Actually, Phoebe found out when she was visiting Caroline while we were in town the other day. I heard you were there when Jerry went after Carl."

"I was. I happened to notice him as I was leaving Carl's cabin. Eric happened to be coming up the hill, so we snuck up behind Jerry together. It was a close one. We almost didn't make it in time."

After a long moment passed between them, Abe asked, "Is it true that Carl is getting a mail-order bride?"

"Yes. He gave me the missive for the stagecoach driver when he came to get the mail." When Abe let out a sigh, Travis asked, "Is something wrong?"

Abe shook his head. "When isn't something wrong when it comes to Carl?" He turned to the basket and picked it up. Then he retrieved the rifle. "I think I have enough for today. Let's get your horses in the barn so they can have some hay to eat."

It was on the tip of Travis' tongue to ask Abe if he was glad Carl was still alive, but in the end, he decided to keep his mouth shut. He knew there were bad feelings between Abe and Carl, and he knew it had to do with the stream that bordered their properties. But he also knew it was best if he kept neutral on the matter. Their problems were better off between them. He had enough to deal with without taking sides, especially when he liked both men. They had, after all, always treated him like he was an ordinary person instead of the monster the townsfolk had claimed him to be.

"So," Abe began as they headed to the barn, "I hear you have a full house now between Allie and Jerry's girls."

Travis chuckled. "Yeah, I suppose you could say that. The cottage seemed a lot bigger before they all came to live with me."

"I bet it doesn't seem so empty, though."

"No, it doesn't. It's better this way."

"How are the girls taking it?"

"As well as can be expected," Travis replied. "They cry from time to time, but I think it'll help that they have each other and their dog."

"I really wish it hadn't been Jerry who killed Lydia," Abe said. "He was one of the few good men in town."

"I think we all have a weakness. I don't think either of us really knows how bad Lydia was."

"No, I don't think we do."

Carl was probably the only one who knew the extent of Lydia's wickedness, but he kept it to himself. Maybe there were some things too hard to discuss.

"They say you don't really know someone until you live with them," Abe said. "Maybe it's a sign that we should be glad we ended up with the women we did. Even if we don't have a lot, we have wives that aren't anything like Lydia."

"Thankfully, they aren't."

And that made Travis love Allie all the more. The next time he saw Eric, he would have to thank him for making him marry the most wonderful woman in the world.

Epilogue

One month later

"Your mother sent a letter," Travis called out to the girls who were playing in the yard with the dog.

Allie glanced up from the flowerbed she'd been tending to and joined the girls and dog as they rushed over to him. He got down from his wagon and handed the missive to the oldest since she could read better than the younger one.

"We'll work on writing a reply after supper," Allie told the girls as she removed her gloves. "I'm sure your mother's anxious to hear from you."

"We miss her," Lilly said, holding the letter to her chest as if it might disappear if she wasn't careful.

"She misses you, too," Allie replied.

While Lilly and Janice sat on the lawn to read the letter, Travis gestured to the wagon full of grocery items. "I got everything you asked for."

"Are you sure you're comfortable going into town?" Allie asked, lowering her voice so the girls wouldn't overhear.

"No, I'm not," he admitted. There was no point in lying. A lifetime of being the object of ridicule wasn't going to go away overnight. But… "It wasn't as bad as I thought it'd be. Ida even came up to talk to me. She asked how the girls are doing, and I told her they're doing well, all things considered. Then I thought since she's the girls' aunt that it'd be good for them if she came out here with Mike and their children."

Allie's eyes grew wide. "You invited all of them over here?"

"Do you mind?" Now that he thought about it, that would make for a lot of food for poor Allie to make.

"No, I don't mind. I'm just surprised you'd do that."

"Well, I am nervous, but it'll be good for Lilly and Janice. And Ida was nice to me. She did go out of her way to approach me in town right where everyone could see her."

"I think Ida's got a good heart."

He nodded. "She does. And she's brave, too."

Allie chuckled. "Brave?"

"It takes a lot of courage to approach someone with my reputation in broad daylight where everyone else can see you."

"I'd approach you if you were in town," she told him, her eyes twinkling.

He put his arm around her shoulders and kissed her. "Yes, I know you would. You have a lot more courage than anyone else."

"Courage has nothing to do with it. I'm proud of you, Travis, and I'm glad you're my husband."

"There's nothing like a good woman to make a man the best he can be." He smiled then turned to the groceries in the wagon. "I'll bring these in, and you can put them where they belong."

"Alright. And after you finish with that, you can get started on a bassinet."

He was in the middle of grabbing one of the wooden crates full of staple items when her meaning registered in his mind. "A bassinet?"

She shot him a wide grin. "Well, you don't need to get started on it right away if you don't want to. The baby won't be here for another eight months."

"Baby? Really?"

"Well, sure. What did you think we were working on when we're in bed?"

He chuckled at her joke. "I'll get started on it today. It'll be fun to make things for a baby."

She gave him a kiss and hugged him. "I love you, Travis."

"I love you, too." Excited by the prospect of making things for a baby, he hurried to unload the wagon.

Coming Next in the Chance at Love Series

Due out January 7, 2017!

Book 4

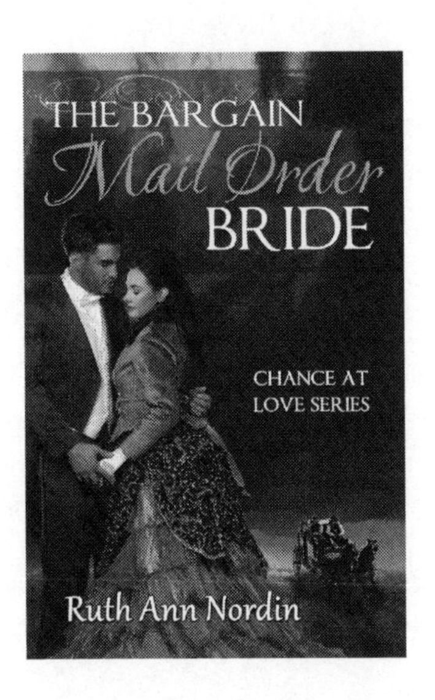

Carl Richie's wife took delight in making him miserable, often reminding him she wished she'd married someone much more deserving. So when she dies, it's no great loss. His problems, however, are far from over.

His father left him twenty acres and a stream that most likely has gold in it, but in order for him to keep the property, he must have a child. The last thing Carl wants to do is marry again, but he has no choice. So, with reluctance, he posts a mail-order bride ad.

Juliet Gilbert needs to marry someone—and fast. On a whim, she answers the first mail-order bride ad that will take her to a place where her past won't catch up with her. From the beginning, Carl makes it clear he's not interested in love. He only wants a child, and then he'll give her a portion of any gold he finds on his land and leave her alone to do as she wishes.

Since love is the least of her concerns, she agrees as long as he never asks about her past. The two strike the bargain, and she comes out to marry him. What neither expects, however, is that bargains are far easier to make than they are to keep.

Don’t miss the other books in the Chance at Love Series!

Book 1

When Phoebe Durbin answers a mail-order bride ad, she doesn't realize the groom-to-be didn't post it. Worse, the day she arrives at her destination, she learns he doesn't even want to get married. Having nowhere else to go, she convinces him to give her a chance to prove having a woman cook and clean for him will be the best thing that ever happened to him.

Abe Thomas reluctantly agrees to take Phoebe in, though he doubts they will make a good match. They're much too different. While she sees the best in things, he knows the world is much darker than she can ever imagine. No woman in her right mind would be his convenient wife. He's sure when the stagecoach comes back to town, she'll be the first one on it. After all, two people so completely different can't make a good match, can they?

Book 2

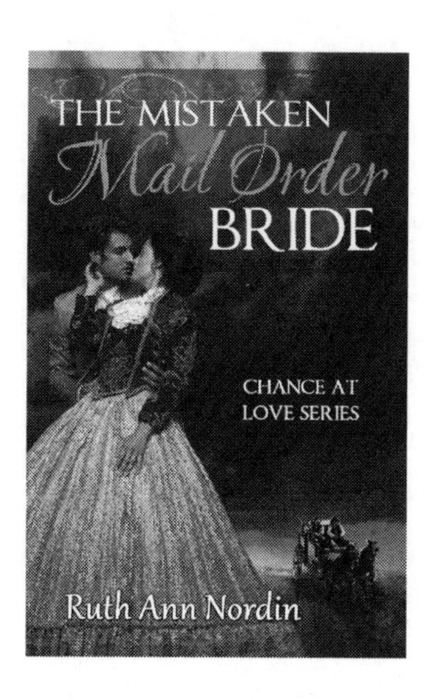

Eric Johnson has been writing to his mail-order bride for months, and at long last, the day she's due to arrive has come. Only, the young lady who comes off the stagecoach isn't at all what he expected. She's homely in appearance, and she has an orphan child with her.

However, he is a man of his word, so he's going to marry her. He had enjoyed their correspondence over the past year, after all, and really, initial impressions aren't everything. But when the preacher pronounces them husband and wife, he finds out she's the wrong lady.

Caroline Benton's just as shocked as he is, not realizing she'd gotten off at the wrong town and followed the wrong man home. Why, oh why, didn't she think to ask him his name? Now she and the orphan child she brought with her are stuck in a strange town with a man who'd been waiting for someone else.

She can't imagine he's at all happy to be paired up with her for the rest of his life. Not only is she rather unattractive, but she doesn't know the first thing about housekeeping. Just what is she supposed to do to convince him it's not the end of the world that he married the wrong mail-order bride?

All Books by Ruth Ann Nordin

(Chronological Order)

Regencies

Marriage by Scandal
The Earl's Inconvenient Wife
A Most Unsuitable Earl
His Reluctant Lady
The Earl's Scandalous Wife

Marriage by Deceit
The Earl's Secret Bargain
Love Lessons With the Duke
Ruined by the Earl
The Earl's Stolen Bride

Marriage by Arrangement
His Wicked Lady
Her Devilish Marquess
The Earl's Wallflower Bride

Standalone Regency
Her Counterfeit Husband

Historical Western Romances

Pioneer Series
Wagon Trail Bride
The Marriage Agreement

Nebraska Series
Her Heart's Desire
A Bride for Tom
A Husband for Margaret

Eye of the Beholder
The Wrong Husband
Shotgun Groom
To Have and To Hold
His Redeeming Bride
Isaac's Decision

Chance at Love Series
The Convenient Mail Order Bride
The Mistaken Mail Order Bride
The Accidental Mail Order Bride

South Dakota Series
Loving Eliza
Bid for a Bride
Bride of Second Chances

Montana Collection
Mitch's Win
Boaz's Wager
Patty's Gamble

Native American Romance Series
Restoring Hope
A Chance In Time
Brave Beginnings
Bound by Honor, Bound by Love

Virginia Series
An Unlikely Place for Love
The Cold Wife
An Inconvenient Marriage
Romancing Adrienne

Historical Romance Anthologies (with Janet Syas Nitsick)
Bride by Arrangement

A Groom's Promise

Standalone Historical Western Romances
Falling In Love With Her Husband
Kent Ashton's Backstory (Prequel to Catching Kent)
Catching Kent
His Convenient Wife
Meant To Be
The Mail Order Bride's Deception

Contemporary Romances

Omaha Series
With This Ring, I Thee Dread
What Nathan Wants
Just Good Friends

Across the Stars Series
Suddenly a Bride
Runaway Bride
His Abducted Bride

Standalone Contemporaries
Substitute Bride
Bride by Design (under pen name Barbara Joan Russell)

Thriller

Return of the Aliens (Christian End-Times Novel)
Late One Night (flash fiction)

Fantasy

Enchanted Galaxy Series
A Royal Engagement

Royal Hearts
The Royal Pursuit
Royal Heiress

Nonfiction

Writing Tips Series
11 Tips for New Writers
The Emotionally Engaging Character

Made in the USA
San Bernardino, CA
19 April 2017